憂鬱少年的藍色希臘

A N G E R I N T H E S U N

Antoinette Moses 著

李樸良 譯

ABOUT THIS BOOK

For the Student 🎧 Listen to the story and do some activities on your Audio APP.
🗨 Talk about the story.

For the Teacher

Go to our Readers Resource site for information on using readers and downloadable Resource Sheets, photocopiable Worksheets, and Tapescripts. www.helblingreaders.com

For lots of great ideas on using Graded Readers consult Reading Matters, the Teacher's Guide to using Helbling Readers.

Structures

Modal verb would	Non-defining relative clauses
I'd love to …	Present perfect continuous
Future continuous	Used to / would
Present perfect future	Used to / used to doing
Reported speech / verbs / questions	Second conditional
Past perfect	Expressing wishes and regrets
Defining relative clauses	

Structures from lower levels are also included.

CONTENTS

When did you first know you wanted to write?

I can't remember a time when I didn't want to write. I first wrote a play, which I performed with my family at Christmas, when I was eight years old. Even when I did other things I always knew I was a writer and I was just filling in time until I could sit down and write.

You mention plays. Do you still write plays or just stories?

I write lots of stories for English language learners and I also write plays as I like the challenge of describing people through what they say and do. It's very different from writing fiction, but very exciting when you see actors playing characters you have invented.

How do you begin a story?

Well I don't wait for inspiration. Often I begin with an issue, for example something that makes me angry or worried. Then I think about the characters. Who would be involved in this issue? What kind of people are affected or get involved in it?

Why did you write this story?

I often begin with a "what if" situation. What if you arrived at the airport and there was no one to meet you? That's how I started this story. Then I got to know Jake and started to think about who he was and what he wanted. The story is always about character rather than plot.

Have you been to Greece?

I lived in Athens for four years and often go to Crete, which is a wonderful island. I know many of the places in the story and they are very dramatic. You can imagine things happening there.

BEFORE READING

1 The story, *Danger in the Sun,* takes place in Athens and on the island of Crete. How much do you know about Athens and Crete? Do the quiz and find out.

1. Who was the city of Athens named after?

   a) A king   b) A goddess   c) A queen

2. When were the first modern Olympic Games held in Athens?

   a) 1796   b) 1886   c) 1996

3. What is the Parthenon?

   a) A castle   b) A park   c) A temple

4. When was it built?

   a) 447-438 BC   b) 1430-1440 AD   c) 1110-1000 BC

⁵ What is the Acropolis?

ⓐ A castle in Athens   ⓑ A hill in Athens   ⓒ A bridge in Athens

⁶ What is the capital city of Crete?

ⓐ Melissa   ⓑ Athens   ⓒ Heraklion

⁷ Which is the largest Greek island?

ⓐ Rhodes   ⓑ Crete   ⓒ Corfu

2 Choose one of the following subjects. Find out more about it. Then give a presentation to the class.

The Acropolis
Athena
The origins of the Olympic Games
The Parthenon

3 Match the words from the book to their definitions.

_____ ① a high rock face, often over the sea   ⓐ vines

_____ ② small rivers   ⓑ rundown

_____ ③ a part of the coast where the land curves inwards   ⓒ ravines

          ⓓ islands

_____ ④ in bad condition   ⓔ bay

_____ ⑤ a small green and black fruit that produces oil   ⓕ olive

          ⓖ cliff

_____ ⑥ plants that produce grapes   ⓗ streams

_____ ⑦ deep narrow valleys with steep sides

_____ ⑧ pieces of land surrounded by water

4 Now try to fit them into the description of Crete from the story.

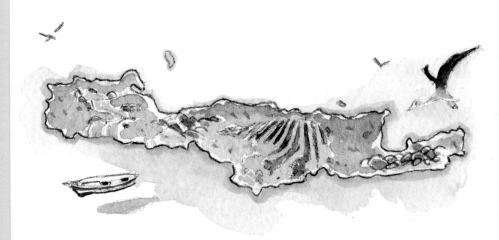

Crete is not what I expected. It's not like other (1)_____
It's bigger, for one thing and it keeps changing. The house
in Panormou is on a steep (2)_____ above a tiny
(3)_____ where the sea is deep green, but in other places
there are just long beaches and the sea is an incredibly deep
blue. As we drive south, it changes. There are little villages
and deep (4)_____ with racing (5)_____ that remind
me of home, and then miles of rocky mountainside that looks
like the surface of the moon. We're driving through a valley of
grape (6)_____ and (7)_____ trees and a scattering
of (8)_____ houses when I see a familiar face.

5 Now try and find a picture of this place in the book.

6 In pairs choose a picture from the book and write a
description. Then describe the picture to another pair.
See if they can guess which picture it is.

7 Look quickly at the pictures in the book. Then answer
the questions.

1 What kind of story is it? Tick.
☐ thriller   ☐ science fiction   ☐ horror   ☐ romance

2 What do you think happens in the story? Tick two items.
☐ a murder   ☐ smuggling
☐ an accident at sea   ☐ a disappearance

8 The main character in the story is a 15-year-old boy called Jake. Where is he in these pictures? Invent a story to connect the pictures. Tell a partner.

9 Write your story and swap with another pair. What happens next? Continue their story.

10 Match the words from the story to the photographs.

_____ a compass   _____ e pottery
_____ b earth paintings _____ f padlocks
_____ c cliffs   _____ g cave
_____ d rope   _____ h tabloids

11 The words are all important to the story. Use each of the words above to complete the sentences.

a That morning, Susie Parsons made a _____ vase.

b It was dark inside the _____ .

c Alex Wyatt used the _____ readings to locate the place.

d The kidnappers tied Nat and Jake's hands and feet with _____ .

e The doors were locked and there were large _____ on them.

f There are pictures of Phil Dawson in the _____ every day.

g When they switched on the torch, they saw _____ on the walls.

h They had to climb down the steep _____ to escape.

12 Choose one of the sentences above. Continue the story from there.

13 Scan pages 15 to 17 of the story to answer the questions below. Ask and answer with a partner.

- a In his fantasy, where is Jake standing with his father?
- b What does Jake's father have a passion for?
- c What is Jake's father's name?
- d When was the last time Jake saw his father?
- e Where is Jake's father supposed to meet him?
- f What is terrible in Athens?
- g Where is the Parliament in Athens?
- h What can you see from Jake's hotel?

14 Listen to the extracts from the book. Then make predictions. Guess the answers to the questions.

a) Why hasn't Jake's father come to meet him? What has happened?

b) What does Jake find in the hotel room?

c) What do you think Natalie will be like?

d) Where are they and what do they find inside?

e) What will happen next?

15 Compare answers with a partner.

This is the fantasy[1]. I am in Athens[2] with my father. Where? Maybe the Parthenon[3]. Yes, I am standing in the middle of the Acropolis[4] with my father. OK, I know you're not allowed to stand there because they are repairing it. This is my fantasy, OK? So I'm there and although I've seen it a thousand times on posters[5] and postcards, it seems quite different.

It is the same, but not exactly the same. I love the place and how old it is and suddenly I understand why my father is an archaeologist[6].

Then he looks at me and he sees all of this in my expression[7] and I know he is really happy. I know that this is what he has always wanted—to share his passion[8] for Greece[9] with his son.

"I guess you've been up here hundreds of times," I say.

"Maybe dozens," he replies. "In the old days it was free entry[10] on Sundays and evenings when there was a full moon. We often came up here with a bottle of wine and we drank and toasted[11] the glories of Ancient[12] Greece."

"In the old days," I joke.

"Yeah," he says. "When dinosaurs[13] walked the earth."

It is our joke. We have jokes. We do things together.

I have many fantasies about my father, Alexander Wyatt. This is one of them.

---

1 fantasy [ˋfæntəsɪ] (n.) 幻想
2 Athens [ˋæθɪnz] (n.) 雅典（希臘首都）
3 Parthenon [ˋpɑrθə,nɑn] (n.) 帕德嫩神殿（希臘雅典女神雅典娜的神殿，建於西元前五世紀）
4 Acropolis [əˋkrɑpəlɪs] (n.) 雅典衛城（築有帕德嫩神殿）
5 poster [ˋpostɚ] (n.) 海報
6 archaeologist [ˌɑrkɪˋɑlədʒɪst] (n.) 考古學家
7 expression [ɪkˋsprɛʃən] (n.) 表情
8 passion [ˋpæʃən] (n.) 熱情
9 Greece [gris] (n.) 希臘
10 entry [ˋɛntrɪ] (n.) 進入；入場
11 toast [tost] (v.) 舉杯祝飲
12 ancient [ˋenʃənt] (a.) 古代的
13 dinosaur [ˋdaɪnə,sɔr] (n.) 恐龍

I have not seen my father for five years. I was ten when he left home. But here I am at Athens airport and, finally, after all this time we are going to have a holiday together. We will visit the Acropolis and he'll show me amazing[1] things and we will have jokes together. Except . . .

Except I am here at Athens airport and he isn't. He isn't here to meet me and I don't know why.

Waiting

- Why do you think Mr Wyatt is not there to meet his son?
- Have you ever waited for someone who arrived very late or didn't turn up[2] ? How did you feel? What did you do?

I take out the last email he sent me. "I am so pleased you're coming here at last. I'll be at the airport to meet you at 14:20."

But now it is 15:30 and I'm standing in a crowd[3] of people with cards saying "Mr Jones" and "Olympic Hotel" and I decide that I don't want to spend my holiday hanging around Athens airport with a lot of strangers. What I want is my dad and just like every other time in my life when I've wanted him, he's not here and I feel really angry and fed up[4].

1 amazing [əˈmezɪŋ] (a.) 驚人的
2 turn up 出現
3 crowd [kraʊd] (n.) 人群
4 be fed up 受夠了；忍無可忍了
5 I'm not in the mood for 我並不想⋯⋯

6 excuse [ɪkˈskjuz] (n.) 藉口
7 information desk 詢問處
8 sharply [ˈʃɑrplɪ] (adv.) 嚴厲地
9 loudspeaker [ˈlaʊdˈspikɚ] (n.) 擴聲器
10 delay [dɪˈle] (v.) 延遲；延誤

When I was ten and I wanted him, I used to tell myself stories. But I'm not ten any more and I am not in the mood for[5] stories. I am going to find my father and I'm going to tell him that when his only son comes to visit after five years he needs a very good excuse[6] when he doesn't turn up. A very, very good excuse.

Then I act. I go to the information desk[7] where a pretty, dark-haired girl smiles at me and says that she is sorry that my father is not there. She then says quite sharply[8] over the loudspeaker[9]: "Alexander Wyatt must come immediately to Information where his son Jake is waiting."

And when he does not come, she looks worried and asks if I am OK. I tell her that I'm fine and that I'll go to the hotel and wait for him there. So she smiles again and says that the traffic in Athens is terrible and he must be delayed[10].

I change some money and I get the metro[11] to Syntagma Square[12] which is where the Parliament[13] is and also (as the nice girl at the information desk showed me) two minutes' walk from my hotel. According to my father, the best thing about the hotel is the view of the Acropolis from the roof. When I get there, I find that my father does have a room for us and that he has talked to the receptionist[14] about my arrival[15] and that he is happy that I am finally coming to Greece.

"I do not understand why he was not at the airport," the receptionist says and looks worried. "He left here three hours ago because he did not want to be late."

11 metro [ˈmɛtro] (n.) 地下鐵
12 Syntagma Square 憲法廣場
（希臘首都雅典的主要廣場）
13 parliament [ˈpɑrləmənt] (n.) 議會
14 receptionist [rɪˈsɛpʃənɪst] (n.) 接待員
15 arrival [əˈraɪvl] (n.) 到達

🎧 The receptionist gives me the key to our room and I go upstairs. When I go in, I find a small case and some clothes that must belong to the man that I call my father. But I don't know, because I haven't seen him for five years.

I feel as if I am in the room of a stranger. What makes me really angry is that I can hear my mother's voice in my head and she is saying: "You see, Jake, I was right. Your father doesn't care about you. You can't rely on¹ him."

But I don't want to believe her. I want to believe that my father does care, but something unexpected has happened. So I tell myself if I go for a swim in the pool on the roof, then he will arrive and we'll go and visit the Acropolis and joke together like a father and a son.

So I go for a swim and there is a great view of the Acropolis which does look like a postcard, and different at the same time. But my father does not arrive.

I ring² his mobile phone³ again (and again and again) but it is not switched on⁴. Why? It doesn't make sense. I know my father wants to see me. Or is this all some terrible way of getting back at⁵ my mother? No. That can't be it. My mother would be really happy to prove that my father was unreliable⁶.

The reason I am here now is because after four years and ten months I discovered that every time my mother said: "Your father isn't interested in you," she was lying.

I discovered this on my birthday when I woke up early and was the first to get to the post⁷.

1 rely on sb 仰靠某人	5 get back at sb 報復某人
2 ring [rɪŋ] (v.) 打電話	6 unreliable [ˌʌnrɪˈlaɪəbl̩]
3 mobile phone [ˈmobɪl fon] 手機	(a.) 靠不住的
4 switch on (機器電器等) 開啟	7 post [post] (n.) 郵箱

Lying on the hall[1] carpet was a letter from my father. That's the same letter that I am reading now as I sit in a hotel in the middle of Athens and look at the linen[2] jacket in the wardrobe[3] and think: "That's my father's jacket. He wears linen jackets."

The letter says—I can tell you without reading it because I've read it so many times:

Dear Jake,

Happy birthday. Fifteen. I imagine you must be almost as tall as I am now, yet I still see you in my mind as the small boy in corduroy[4] trousers that I last saw so many years ago. And I suppose you still don't want to hear from me, as your mother says in her letters, but I'm going to write to you again, just as I always do on your birthday and at Christmas because you are my son and I love you very much and miss you. I hope that one day you will be able to forgive[5] me and we will meet up again. And maybe I can show you a little bit of Greece and we can begin to discover each other. So I hope that this year you won't send this letter back to me unread[6] . . .

1 hall [hɔl] (n.) 大廳
2 linen [ˈlɪnən] (a.) 亞麻布的
3 wardrobe [ˈwɔrd,rob] (n.) 衣櫥
4 corduroy [ˌkɔrdəˈrɔɪ] (a.) 燈芯絨的
5 forgive [fəˈgɪv] (v.) 原諒（動詞三態：forgive; forgave; forgiven）
6 unread [ʌnˈrɛd] (a.) 未讀取的

And it was at this point that I started to shout at my mother and ask her what she had done and how could she have done it? And we had a huge row[7] which went on for days. And my mother cried and said I didn't understand, and I told her that she didn't understand. My father wrote to me every year and I didn't know. I still can't forgive her.

It was not as if my father was a criminal[8]. He was an archaeologist who had an affair with[9] another young archaeologist and my mother found out and threw him out[10] of the house. And she told him that he was never going to see me again. As if I was just something to use in a row. As if I didn't have feelings or wants. As if growing up thinking your father didn't care was OK, which it wasn't.

---

7 row [ro] (n.) 口角；爭吵
8 criminal [ˈkrɪmənl] (n.) 罪犯
9 have an affair with sb 和某人鬧緋聞
10 throw sb out 把某人轟出門（動詞三態：throw; threw; thrown）

Secrets

- Jake's mum keeps his father's letters a secret from him. Why do you think she does this?
- Have you ever kept a secret from someone? Why did you decide to do this?

After the rows I phoned my father and we had an amazing long talk. Then we emailed each other and he invited me to come to Greece for the summer. My mother was so angry she could hardly speak to me. So she decided to spend the summer at some yoga[1] place in Scotland where she could find herself. Or that was what she said.

And so here I am in Greece at last. But I'm still without my father. And I have no idea where my mother is. I don't think she gave me the name of the yoga place, though I do remember she said it was very peaceful and it didn't even have a phone. And it is now about eight in the evening and I still don't know what has happened to my father.

At nine o'clock the receptionist thinks that maybe my father had an accident and he rings the police and asks them to contact[2] the hospitals. But he is not in any hospital, so the receptionist thinks that maybe he met a friend and went for a drink. Is my father a drunk[3]? Is that what he is saying? But the receptionist says no, that is not what he is saying. It was a suggestion.

1 yoga [ˈjogə] (n.) 瑜珈
2 contact [kənˈtækt] (v.) 聯絡
3 drunk [drʌŋk] (n.) 酒鬼
4 bit [bɪt] (n.) 小片；小塊
5 vendor [ˈvɛndɚ] (n.) 小販
6 tourist [ˈtʊrɪst] (n.) 觀光客
7 canopy [ˈkænəpɪ] (n.) 頂篷；遮蓋物
8 vine [vaɪn] (n.) 藤蔓

"Why don't you go for a walk round the Plaka and enjoy the city? Then tomorrow morning I am sure he will be here," he says.

So I walk round the Plaka looking at bits[4] of old stone and I eat a cheese pie from a street vendor[5]. There are tourists[6] eating dinner in little restaurants under canopies[7] of vines[8] and they all look so happy. I hate them and I hate my father. Why is he doing this to me?

Then I go to bed and, in the morning, of course, he is not here. So the receptionist suggests that I talk to the tourist police.

The police station is incredibly[9] noisy. It is full of shouting or crying tourists and the general scenario[10] seems to be that either the tourists have lost their money, passports, tickets, or all of these, or they have gone for a walk and can't remember the name of their hotel. The tourist police are incredibly patient[11].

"But all my holiday money was inside it." The woman in the queue[12] in front of me is telling the policeman who has clearly heard it all before. She is about the same age as my mother, but much fatter. She is wearing a long shapeless skirt and a baggy[13] T-shirt and her face is very red.

Holiday Disasters

- Has anything bad ever happened to you or your family on holiday?
- Imagine you are in Jake's situation. What would you do?

---

9 incredibly [ɪnˈkrɛdəblɪ] (adv.) 難以置信地
10 scenario [sɪˈnɛrɪˌo] (n.) 情節
11 patient [ˈpeʃənt] (a.) 耐心的
12 queue [kju] (n.) 長隊
13 baggy [ˈbægɪ] (a.) 寬鬆下垂的

"I come to Greece every year," she says, "but this has never happened to me before. I always feel safe here."

The policeman shrugs[1]. "This is a safe country," he says. "But now there are many foreigners here. If you sit in Syntagma Square you must watch your bag. You do not place it on the back of your chair."

Then it is my turn and the policeman listens to me and it is clear that he thinks I am inventing a story.

"Your father is missing?" he asks me. And I explain.

"Perhaps he forgot."

I tell him that my father came from Crete[2] to meet me and that his clothes are in the hotel.

"And the name of the hotel?" he asks.

"The Electra Palace," I say.

He looks slightly[3] surprised. I clearly don't look smart[4] enough to be the kind of person who stays in such a good hotel.

He telephones the hotel and then goes to talk to a colleague.

"We telephoned all the hospitals yesterday," he says. "Your father is not in a hospital. I do not understand what you want us to do."

I'm not sure either. Well, I want them to find my father, but they don't look like the kind of police who race out in fast cars and behave like the FBI[5] in one of those missing[6] persons films[7].

---

1 shrug [ʃrʌg] (v.) 聳肩
2 Crete [krit] (n.) 克里特島
  （希臘的第一大島）
3 slightly [ˈslaɪtlɪ] (adv.) 有一點兒
4 smart [smɑrt] (a.) 時髦的

5 FBI 美國聯邦調查局（Federal Bureau of Investigation）
6 missing [ˈmɪsɪŋ] (a.) 失蹤的
7 film [fɪlm] (n.) 軟片；電影

"Look," I begin again. "My father is the archaeologist Alexander Wyatt. Yesterday afternoon he left the hotel to meet my flight. Now he is missing. Surely you can do something?"

I want to add that I am lost, too. I don't know how to contact my mother, I don't know what to do, but I don't want to sound like a small child. But it seems that I've said a magic word.

"Archaeologist?" says the policeman. "I understand. Come with me."

I don't understand anything and he's not explaining. But at least he hasn't sent me away[1]. He takes me to a small room and tells me to sit down. Then he shuts the door and leaves.

There is not much in the room, a low coffee table covered in rings from coffee cups, three old plastic[2] chairs and two gray filing cabinets[3]. This is a great way to begin my holiday, I think.

"Come on, Jake," I say to myself. "Be positive. Something important turned up at work. Maybe they made an amazing discovery and Alex had to be there. And he's going to rush in, covered in earth and he will be so sorry and yet really excited and he'll take me to see what he has found."

Or perhaps he is just very absent-minded[4] and the police will find him in a dusty room in the museum . . . but I stop myself continuing this fantasy as my father didn't seem at all forgetful on the phone or in his emails.

I am going round in circles[5] and getting nowhere.

---

1 send sb away 打發某人
2 plastic [ˈplæstɪk] (a.) 塑膠的
3 cabinet [ˈkæbənɪt] (n.) 櫃子
4 absent-minded [ˈæbsəntˌmaɪndɪd] (a.) 心不在焉的
5 circle [ˈsɝkl̩] (n.) 圓圈
6 reply [rɪˈplaɪ] (v.) 回覆
7 branch [bræntʃ] (n.) 分部；分支
8 civilization [ˌsɪvləˈzeʃən] (n.) 文明
9 treasure [ˈtrɛʒɚ] (n.) 寶藏

I check my phone again for messages but there is only one from Pete, who is my best friend at school. I begin to reply[6] but then the door opens and it isn't Dad, but another policeman who says his name is Nikos Filosomething and he is with the archaeology branch[7] of the police. He is younger than the first policeman, and looks more efficient. He clearly doesn't like me, but I'm not sure why.

"So, what is your father working on at the moment?" he asks.

I say I don't know and explain why. He looks surprised, but says nothing.

"Archaeology police?" I ask.

"Here in Greece we have the beginning of civilization[8] and some of the greatest treasures[9] in the world and many people want to steal them. Like our Venus from Milos[10] and the great Marbles[11] which your Lord Elgin took to London."

VENUS FROM MILOS

10 Venus from Milos 米洛的維納斯
（即知名的斷臂維納斯）
11 Marbles [ˋmɑrblz] (n.) 埃爾金大
理石雕（Elgin Marbles，從帕德
嫩神廟被盜出）

"Do you think my father found someone stealing something?"

"I do not know," says Nikos. "But there is always this possibility I will naturally contact the British Archaeology School in Crete . . ."

"I think he has an office here, too," I say.

"The British School," he replies. "I know them. You say his luggage is in the hotel. Have you looked through his belongings[1]? Are there any papers or anything that says where he has gone?"

"No," I say.

I looked at his case all last night, but it felt wrong to look through his things. I hardly know him, after all. But this morning I was so fed up I finally opened it and looked inside. And there weren't any papers, nothing, in fact, that told me anything about my father. I'm not sure what I hoped to find: a diary[2], his laptop[3]? Did he have his laptop with him? I didn't know. There was just the usual stuff[4], a wash bag, a sweater. And . . .

Belongings

- What can you tell about a person from his/her belongings?
- What things have you got in your bag?

1 belongings [bə'lɔŋɪŋz] (n.) 〔複〕所攜帶之物
2 diary ['daɪərɪ] (n.) 日記
3 laptop ['læptɑp] (n.) 筆記型電腦
4 stuff [stʌf] (n.) 東西
5 clay [kle] (n.) 黏土
6 faint [fent] (a.) 微弱的
7 marking ['mɑrkɪŋ] (n.) 斑紋
8 weigh [we] (v.) 稱……的重量
9 laboratory ['læbrə,torɪ] (n.) 實驗室
10 analyze ['ænḷ,aɪz] (v.) 分析
11 smuggle ['smʌgḷ] (v.) 走私
12 irritated ['ɪrə,tetɪd] (a.) 煩躁的

"Actually there was this," I tell Nikos.

I show him a small piece of rock. It's the color of clay[5] but it has some faint[6] markings[7] on it which are a dark red.

Nikos takes it and weighs[8] it in his hand. "It may be something and it may be nothing," he says. "I'm not an expert like your father. But I will send it to the laboratories[9] so they can analyze[10] the paint. It may be old. Perhaps your father has made an interesting new discovery."

He sounds as if this is most unlikely.

"Do you think someone wants to smuggle[11] it out of Greece?"

"All things are possible. But there may be a very simple explanation. We shall see." He smiles, or at least his mouth smiles.

His eyes look cold. He looks irritated[12] and rather bored.

"In the meantime, I feel you should go home until we find him."

I explain about my mother.

"That is a problem," Nikos says. "You must return to England. I think we must telephone your embassy[1]."

He picks up the phone and talks to several people. I cannot understand anything he is saying except for the name of my father, which he repeats several times. Then he stands up and passes the phone to me.

"It is your ambassador[2]," he says. "It seems that Alexander Wyatt is a good friend of his."

At last I can talk to someone who knows him, I think. I take the phone.

"Is that Jake?" says a kind, educated[3] voice. "John Parsons here. Your father's an old friend of the family. Inspector[4] Filopapos has just told me what's going on. This isn't like Alexander at all. But don't worry, we'll get it all sorted out[5]. I'll call your mother."

I explain. Again.

"Right," says the ambassador. "Well, what about other family?" he asks.

"I've got an aunt in Canada," I say. "My father had a brother who died of measles[6] when he was seven."

"Friends?" asks the ambassador.

I think of Pete. Then I remember that he and his family are in France, but I don't know where exactly.

---

1 embassy ['ɛmbəsɪ] (n.) 大使館
2 ambassador [æm'bæsədɚ] (n.) 大使
3 educated ['ɛdʒuˌketɪd] (a.) 有教養的
4 inspector [ɪn'spɛktɚ] (n.) 督察員

Friends and family

- Who would you contact if you were in Jake's situation?

"Well," says the ambassador. "You'd better come and stay here, then. Susie, that's my wife, will be delighted[7]. And you can be company[8] for our daughter Natalie. How old are you? Sixteen?"

"Almost," I say.

"Not so much difference then. Nat's just eighteen. It will be nice for her to have some company of about the same age."

I wonder if there is any universe[9] where an eighteen-year-old girl finds it nice to be placed in the company of a boy who is not yet quite sixteen. At school the idea of any girl from year twelve[10] wanting to spend time with a year nine or ten is so unlikely it's off the scale[11] of unlikely things. I imagine Natalie is smart and snobby[12] and will hate me instantly[13].

I say goodbye to Inspector Nikos. I am sure that he will do nothing at all to find my father. He promises to tell me the moment he has any news and writes down my mobile number, but I don't expect to hear from him again. As we go through the main office, I see policeman number one with an elderly American.

5 sort out 解決；釐清
6 measles [ˈmizlz] (n.) 麻疹
7 delighted [dɪˈlaɪtɪd] (a.) 高興的
8 company [ˈkʌmpənɪ] (n.) 陪伴
9 universe [ˈjunəˌvɝs] (n.) 宇宙；全世界
10 year twelve〔英國學制〕12 年級
11 off the scale 超出正常的尺度範圍
12 snobby [ˈsnɑbɪ] (a.) 勢利眼的
13 instantly [ˈɪnstəntlɪ] (adv.) 立即

"I just went out for a short walk," the American is saying. "I know there was some kind of sign[1] near the hotel. And there was a café on the other side of the road."

The policeman is trying to look patient. He waves at[2] me as we go past. "I hope you find your father," he says.

Another policeman takes me in to the hotel, where I collect my luggage and Dad's things and pay for the room. The receptionist says how sorry he is and sounds as if he really means it.

Then we drive to the British Embassy, which is this massive[3] building inside a walled[4] garden. This is going to be awful[5], I think. I've only got some jeans and T-shirts with me and I'm sure it's the kind of place where everyone wears suits.

This whole trip is a disaster[6], I think. But just as I walk towards the steps I see a tall slim woman with her hair in a ponytail[7], wearing a pair of very grubby[8] jeans and a huge white shirt covered in smears[9] of red mud.

"Hi," she says. "You must be Jake. I'm Susie. Come on in. You poor boy, what a nightmare[10]. And so unlike Alex. I simply can't think what has happened to him. But we must be positive; it's probably some work thing. Anyhow, you're very welcome here until we get everything sorted out."

She's so friendly I feel as if I've always known her.

---

1 sign [saɪn] (n.) 招牌
2 wave at sb 向某人招手
3 massive ['mæsɪv] (a.) 魁偉的
4 walled [wɔld] (a.) 有圍牆的
5 awful ['ɔful] (a.) 慘的

6 disaster [dɪ'zæstɚ] (n.) 災難
7 ponytail ['ponɪ,tel] (n.) 馬尾辮
8 grubby ['grʌbɪ] (a.) 髒的
9 smear [smɪr] (n.) 污跡
10 nightmare ['naɪt,mɛr] (n.) 惡夢

"Natalie will show you around. She's only been home from boarding school[1] herself for a couple of weeks. Nat!" she shouts over her shoulder. "Natalie's our daughter," she continues. "Now, come in don't just stand there."

We go into a grand[2] entrance[3] hall which is all pillars and marble, like going into a palace. The ceiling has pieces of decorated plaster[4] like a wedding cake and everything echoes[5].

"This is probably the only great formal house left in this part of Athens," Susie continues as she walks, "apart from the Benaki Museum. Costs a fortune[6] to heat in the winter, but at least it's cool in summer. Churchill[7] came here you know in 1944. When he was trying to make sure that Greece didn't fall under the control of the Russians[8] . . . Nat thinks it's haunted[9] . . . don't you, darling?" This last remark[10] is again shouted over her shoulder. "Ghosts and ghouls[11]. Ghouls is what she calls the other ambassadors."

I follow her down a long corridor[12] wondering if she ever stops to breathe.

"Are you hungry?" Susie asks me. "We tend[13] to have lunch late. I like to get most of my work done in the mornings. Did John tell you? I'm a potter[14]. I've got a show coming up next month so I try and find as much time as possible. Here we are . . ." she finishes, as we step inside what looks like an English farmhouse kitchen with a huge pine[15] table and a couple of ancient armchairs occupied by two fat and contented[16] cats.

---

1 boarding school 寄宿學校
2 grand [grænd] (a.) 雄偉的
3 entrance [ˈɛntrəns] (n.) 入口
4 plaster [ˈplæstɚ] (n.) 灰漿
5 echo [ˈɛko] (v.) 發出回聲
6 fortune [ˈfɔrtʃən] (n.) 巨款

"This is where we live. I'd have all our meals here if it was up to me. But we have to fly the flag[17] and do the formal stuff a few times a week. But you don't have to dress up[18] and chat. Nat refuses and I tell her she's right. No one pays[19] her to be the embassy daughter. So she eats in here—when she's in, that is. She's often out in the evenings, clubs and cafés. You know what it's like."

Embassies and Ambassadors

- What is an embassy? Why is it important?
- Who is an ambassador?
- Imagine growing up in an embassy. What would it be like? How would it be different from your life now?

No, I want to tell her. I have no idea what's it's like to grow up in an embassy and go out clubbing[20] with other embassy brats[21]. I live in Chesterfield, which is not exactly the club and café capital of the world. In fact it's probably so far off Nat's social radar that she doesn't even know where it is. I know I am going to really dislike Natalie.

7 Churchill 邱吉爾（英國政治家）
8 Russian [ˈrʌʃən] (n.) 俄國人
9 haunted [ˈhɔntɪd] (a.) 鬧鬼的
10 remark [rɪˈmɑrk] (n.) 談論
11 ghoul [gul] (n.) 食屍鬼；嗜好可怕而古怪的人
12 corridor [ˈkɔrɪdə] (n.) 走廊
13 tend [tɛnd] (v.) 傾向
14 potter [ˈpɑtə] (n.) 陶藝家
15 pine [paɪn] (n.) 松樹
16 contented [kənˈtɛntɪd] (a.) 滿足的
17 fly the flag 搖旗吶喊，指支持自己的國家（或尤其身在國外時）
18 dress up 盛裝打扮
19 pay [pe] (v.) 給予（注意）
20 clubbing [ˈklʌbɪŋ] (n.) 去夜總會
21 brat [bræt] (n.) 頑童；小搗蛋

1 paddock [ˋpædək] (n.) 賽馬場的草地
　圍場（供賽前展示賽馬用）
2 polish [ˋpolɪʃ] (v.) 擦亮
3 grin [grɪn] (v.) 露齒而笑
4 upset [ʌpˋsɛt] (a.) 心煩的
5 Brit [brɪt] (n.) 英國佬

6 wash up 到達
7 calm down 冷靜下來
8 remarkable [rɪˋmɑrkəbl̩] (a.) 非凡的
9 espresso [ɛsˋprɛso] (n.)（用蒸汽加壓
　煮出的）濃咖啡
10 screw [skru] (v.) 擰

And then she walks in. Have you ever seen a race horse walk into a paddock[1]? It looks all shiny as if everyone has been polishing[2] it for days, and it's perfect and beautiful and it looks completely right. It belongs in its space. That's Natalie. And she smiles at me and her smile makes me feel that she's really happy I'm there. And I know that whatever else happens to me in my life, I want Natalie as a friend.

"Hi," she says. "So you're Jake. I expect Mum's been telling you a hundred things all at once and you can't remember one of them."

I grin[3]. Actually I think I'm already grinning. Like the Cheshire Cat in *Alice in Wonderland*. I know I look a complete idiot.

"You look just like your father," Natalie says.

"Do I?" I ask.

"Well, younger . . ." Natalie laughs. "Like some coffee? Or tea. We have to have tea for all the upset[4] Brits[5] who wash up[6] here. A cup of real English tea is what we always give them to calm them down[7]. It's remarkable[8] how effective it is."

"Coffee's fine," I say.

Natalie starts to pour water into one of those complicated Italian espresso[9] things that you screw[10] together and I can't stop thinking how graceful she is when she moves.

"Um . . . Natalie . . ." I begin.

"Nat," she says. "Only strangers call me Natalie."

She doesn't think of me as a stranger!

"Do you know Alex, my father?"

"Of course," says Nat. "We've got a holiday home on Crete and he often comes to stay. Ever since I can remember. I've always known him."

So why didn't he bring Mum and me to Crete? I'm wondering. Nat makes us both coffee and we push the cats off the chairs— much to their disgust[1]—and slump down[2].

"So what are you going to do?" Nat asks me.

"What do you mean?" I say. "What can I do?"

"Well," she demands. "Aren't you going to look for your Dad?"

"No," I say. "How can I? It's up to[3] the police."

"And do you think they're really going to set up[4] a major investigation[5]?"

I don't. I have the feeling that now they are rid of[6] me. They are going to do nothing at all. My own opinion is that they are quite certain that Alex Wyatt did not want to spend the summer with his son and has gone off to some island with a girlfriend. In fact they are probably laughing about it right now. But I don't say any of this to Nat, who I'm beginning to like a little less.

"Well," Nat continues, curling[7] her impossibly long legs under her. "Do you?"

She may be beautiful, but she is beginning to annoy me.

"No." I tell her. "Of course not. I don't think the police will do anything."

"So?"

---

1 disgust [dɪsˈgʌst] (n.) 厭惡
2 slump down 很放鬆地坐下
3 up to sb 決定於某人
4 set up 展開
5 investigation [ɪnˌvɛstəˈgeʃən] (n.) 調查
6 be/get rid of sb 甩開某人

 "So what?" I say. "What can I do?"

"Investigate yourself," says Nat.

She's either bored or mad.

"Really," I say in my deepest voice, trying not to squeak[8], though I am not very successful. "And how do you suggest I do that? I've been in Greece for less than a day. I don't speak a word of Greek and I don't even know what my father looks like."

"You don't know . . ."

"No. I haven't seen him for five years. Satisfied?"

Surprising news

- Jake's news surprises Nat. How do you think he feels? How do you think she feels?
- Have you ever said or heard a piece of surprising news? Describe what happened.

She immediately changes her tone[9].

"Jake, I'm so sorry, I didn't realize. It's just that I like Alex myself so much, and this is just not like him. He's really nice and thoughtful[10]."

"Then why wasn't he at the airport?" I ask her. I am now squeaking.

---

7 curl [kɝl] (v.) 捲曲
8 squeak [skwik] (v.) 以短促尖聲說出
9 tone [ton] (n.) 聲調；語氣
10 thoughtful [ˋθɔtfəl] (a.) 體貼的

"That's what is bothering me," she says. "That's why I think we have to do something." And she sounds as if she really cares.

"We?"

"Well, if you don't speak Greek and don't know your way round Athens, you're going to need me. Or are you just going to sit there drinking coffee like a pudding?"

"Of course not," I say, trying to sound keen[1] and un-pudding like. How can you drink coffee like a pudding? "So where do we start?" I ask.

I doubt if she has any ideas, but at least it will stop her accusing me of[2] doing nothing. I've only been here a few minutes and she makes it sound as if I've been doing nothing for days.

"The last thing we know about Alex is that he took a taxi. So we start there. Most hotels use one taxi company, don't they?"

I'm wrong. She does have ideas. And she's right.

"Of course," I say. "The hotel called a taxi."

"Do you have the number of the hotel?"

I pull out the hotel receipt from my pocket and give it to her.

"I'll use my mobile," she says. "I never know with the phone here how many people are listening."

"Do you think that the embassy phones are bugged[3]?" I ask her.

"Yeah," she says. "They often are. Mum says in the old days if you wanted to tell the government[4] anything you just rang someone, and the information went straight to Syntagma."

---

1 keen [kin] (a.) 熱心的
2 accuse sb of sth 控告某人做了某事
3 bugged [`bʌgɪd] (a.) 被竊聽的
4 government [`gʌvənmənt] (n.) 政府

I feel as if I've walked into a very different world. Nat takes out a slim and very pink mobile and rings the hotel number and chatters⁵ away to someone in what sounds like really good Greek. I mean she doesn't have any English accent⁶ when she speaks Greek.

"Got a pen?" she asks.

I hand her a pen and a bit of paper and she writes down a number.

"Great," she says. And rings it.

This time she gets into an argument⁷ with whoever she's talking to. "They won't put me through to⁸ the driver," she says, putting her hand over the phone.

"How about if we asked for the same driver to take us somewhere?"

"Of course," she says and speaks into the phone again.

"Brilliant⁹," she says as she folds¹⁰ her mobile and puts it into her pocket. "He's coming here after lunch. We can get him to take us to the same place as he took Alex. Now," she adds. "I'd better show you your room."

---

5 chatter [ˈtʃætɚ] (v.) 喋喋不休地說
6 accent [ˈæksɛnt] (n.) 口音；腔調
7 argument [ˈɑrgjəmənt] (n.) 爭論
8 put sb through to sb
　 把某人的電話轉給某人
9 brilliant [ˈbrɪljənt] (a.) 高明的
10 fold [fold] (v.) 摺疊

Lunch is amazing. Not the food, though it's really good, bread and cheeses and a big Greek salad which Susie puts together in about five seconds. But the conversation.

The family all talk non-stop[1] and yet they all seem to hear each other. It couldn't have been less like home, where I'm lucky if Mum and I say ten words to each other. Except on the days when she's angry and shouts.

And they're talking about so many different things. They talk about the pieces that Susie's making for her exhibition[2] and Nat tells her about an exhibition she's seen in London of Aztec[3] pottery[4], then John tells me I mustn't miss the black pots[5] in the National Museum and Nat promises to take me. Later, as they chat about people they know and what they are doing, I sit back and think what it must be like to live in a family like this.

"So, Jake," says Susie, bringing me back into the conversation. "What do you want to do this afternoon?"

"Give the boy a chance[6]," says John.

"We could ring Vassili and see if he could open the back gate of the Acropolis, so Jake could have a look round after all the tourists have gone," suggests Susie. "Then let's go up to the top of Lykavvitos for a drink so he can see the view."

"And see just how polluted[7] and crowded Athens is," says Nat smiling at me. "Maybe he'd rather wait and go round the Acropolis with Alex," she adds.

And I am amazed at how she seems to understand what I'm thinking.

1 non-stop [nɑnˋstɑp] (adv.) 不休息地
2 exhibition [ˌɛksəˋbɪʃən] (n.) 展覽
3 Aztec [ˋæztɛk] (n.) 阿茲特克 (中美洲
  的古文明)
4 pottery [ˋpɑtərɪ] (n.) 陶器
5 pot [pɑt] (n.) 罐
6 give sb a chance 讓某人休息一下
7 polluted [pəˋlutɪd] (a.) 受污染的

Understanding

- Jake feels that Nat understands what he is thinking. Who do you think understands you best?
- Who do you think that you understand best?

(28) "Of course," says Susie. "Why not just pop¹ across the road to the National² Gallery³ or the Byzantine⁴ Museum? It's only a few minutes away."

"Good idea," says John. "There's a rather fine El Greco⁵. You might enjoy seeing it."

I'm about to say that I like El Greco. Mum teaches art, so at least I do know a bit about that, but I can't say anything because Susie is already saying that she thinks it's a workshop⁶ copy because it looks so rushed.

"That's what I like about it," argues John, "the energy. It's much too good to be one of the copies. Anyhow, let Jake decide."

I can't believe that they are talking to me as if I was one of them, and that it was normal for me to drop into exhibitions before drinks.

And while they talk I keep thinking that my life might be like this all the time if I lived with Dad. Then I laugh at myself for the thought. If I lived with Dad . . . as if he wanted that. He didn't even turn up at the airport.

---

1 pop [pɑp] (v.) （迅速地）行動
2 national [ˈnæʃənl] (a.) 國立的
3 gallery [ˈgælərɪ] (n.) 美術館
4 Byzantine [bɪˈzæntɪn] (a.) 拜占庭的
5 El Greco 艾爾・葛雷柯（1541-1614，西班牙文藝復興時期畫家出生於克里特島）

44

It's finally decided that we'll have a lazy day until we meet up this evening and go for a drink. Which fits in[7] well with Nat's and my plans to find out where the taxi took Dad.

*　*　*　*　*　*

The taxi driver is called Spiro. Nat talks to him and in a few minutes he is smiling at her and chatting as if he's known her all his life. Nat reports that my father wanted to go to the airport to meet me, but he was early. So he decided to go to his office first.

"Did he say why?" I ask.

She translates[8] my question.

"No," Nat reports back.

Then Spiro starts to say something and Nat listens and frowns[9].

"Spiro says that when he was outside the British School, he noticed a large black car parked opposite[10]. Just as your dad got out of the car, a man started to get out of the black car. As soon as Alex saw him, he turned and gave Spiro twenty euros[11] and said that he'd forgotten something and that he would get the metro from Evangelismos station. Then Alex ran into the building."

6 workshop [ˈwɝkˌʃɑp] (n.) 工坊
7 fit in 合適
8 translate [trænsˈlet] (v.) 翻譯
9 frown [fraʊn] (v.) 皺眉
10 opposite [ˈɑpəzɪt] (adv.) 在對面
11 euro [ˈjʊro] (n.) 歐元

"And Spiro drove off?" I ask.

"Yes," says Nat. "Your dad didn't even wait for his change."

"So we need to go to the British School and find out where he went next!" I say.

"Yeah," agrees Nat. "It's only a few minutes' walk."

But Spiro, who seems genuinely[1] concerned[2] that Dad is missing, insists on[3] taking us there himself for free.

He stops outside a large neo-classical[4] building and points out where the black car was parked. He gives me his card before he drives off and asks me to phone and let him know when I find my father.

We go into the school where a pretty girl at reception called Vicki tells me that she saw my father come into the building but, now she thinks about it, she didn't see him leave it.

She rings several people and reports back that no one else saw him. It seems he didn't visit anyone or go into the library. If he didn't come out this way, Nat asks, is there any other way out?

"Yes," says Vicki, "he could go out through the garden. But why would he do that?"

Nat and I look at each other and we are both thinking: the man in the black car.

"Can we go that way?" asks Nat. "We'll just go to the gate and come back again?"

1 genuinely [ˋdʒɛnjuɪnlɪ] (adv.) 真誠地
2 concerned [kənˋsɝnd] (a.) 關心的
3 insist on sth 堅持某事
4 neo-classical [ˌnioˋklæsɪkl] (a.) 新古典風格的

"Of course," says Vicki. "Anything to help. This is very strange. I'll call Crete and see if anyone there has heard from him.".

"Could you ask them what he was working on?" says Nat.

"Certainly," says Vicki, "though I can't see how that is relevant[1]."

"Do you know what I'm thinking?" I say as we walk through the garden past a tennis court[2]. "The police asked me if Dad had any papers with him and there weren't any at the hotel, but what if he had them with him?"

"Yes. Or his laptop. He never goes anywhere without that," Nat replies.

"He must have put it somewhere," I say.

We start to look around us. There are trees and a few bushes[3], but nowhere to hide anything. We go down to the gate and then retrace[4] our steps.

"Weren't there cupboards[5] along the wall of the corridor?" I ask, remembering a line of wooden doors.

Quietly, very quietly, we start opening all the cupboards. They are mostly full of files[6] and boxes and books, though one cupboard contains[7] a bottle of tiny[8] pieces of pottery.

"Shards," says Nat. "That's the proper[9] name for small bits of old pottery. Alex says that even though they can't piece them together, they aren't allowed to throw them away." She smiled. "It's not surprising. They're probably over two thousand years old."

I'm tempted[10] to take a tiny piece and put it in my pocket, but then remember why I'm here, so stop myself.

1 relevant [ˈrɛləvənt] (a.) 有關的
2 tennis court 網球場
3 bush [bʊʃ] (n.) 灌木叢
4 retrace [rɪˈtres] (v.) 折回
5 cupboard [ˈkʌbəd] (n.) 碗櫃
6 file [faɪl] (n.) 檔案
7 contain [kənˈten] (v.) 包含
8 tiny [ˈtaɪnɪ] (a.) 微小的
9 proper [ˈprɑpə] (a.) 嚴格意義上的
10 tempt [tɛmpt] (v.) 引誘；打動

"They're not like the bit Dad had with him," I say.

"What bit?" asks Nat.

So I tell her about the small bit of rough stone with the red paint and she frowns.

"It doesn't sound like anything I've ever seen," she says. "Pottery is usually very smooth[1]."

Three worryingly[2] squeaky[3] cupboards later we find it. His laptop is in a canvas[4] bag that Nat recognizes immediately. She knows so much more about him than I do.

We thank Vicki and say goodbye. She doesn't notice that Nat has now got another bag, and says that she'll phone the embassy if she has any news about my father.

We walk back down the steep road to the embassy trying to look cool. All I can think about is the laptop. I can't wait to look inside it. I'm sure it will give us a real clue[5].

I'm beginning to think that Nat is right and that something has happened to Dad. That it isn't that he didn't want to see me. But it's not a very happy feeling, because if he was OK, he'd ring me. Wouldn't he? It's all very odd. Who was the man in the black car and why did Dad run away from him?

Susie and John are both working, so there is no one in the family kitchen. The family kitchen is a room that Susie has designed, where the family can come to pretend they don't live in an embassy.

---

1 smooth [smuð] (a.) 平滑的
2 worryingly [ˈwɜɪŋlɪ] (adv.) 令人煩惱地
3 squeaky [ˈskwikɪ] (a.) 發短促尖聲的
4 canvas [ˈkænvəs] (a.) 帆布製的

 The laptop, of course has a password[6] and we have no idea what it is. We try the names of a few archaeological sites on Crete: Knossos, Phaistos, Gortys, and Nat googles[7] a few more and comes up with[8] Armeni and Phylaki. But it's no good.

Passwords

- Can you guess the password to Jake's father's laptop?
- Have you got any passwords? How do you decide your passwords?

"This is hopeless," I say. "It could be anything."

But before we can go on trying different names, we hear voices and phones ringing. Then both John and Susie come in. We close the laptop quickly, but they are too busy to notice what we are doing.

"Jake, Nat," cries Susie. "Thank goodness you're both here. There's a bit of a crisis[9]."

"What's happened?" asks Nat. "Is it a bomb?"

"No, no, nothing like that," says her dad reassuringly[10]. "It's just some stupid English footballer[11]."

"Who?" asks Nat.

---

5 clue [klu] (n.) 線索
6 password [ˈpæsˌwɝd] (n.) 密碼
7 google [ˈgugl] (v.) 上網搜尋
8 come up with (針對問題等) 想出

9 crisis [ˈkraɪsɪs] (n.) 危機
10 reassuringly [ˌriəˈʃurɪŋlɪ] (adv.) 安慰地
11 footballer [ˈfutˌbɔlɚ] (n.) 足球運動員

🎧 "Phil Dawson," says Susie, naming the current[1] English captain, a man who is featured[2] in almost every tabloid[3] newspaper on a daily basis.

"It seems that he was holidaying on a yacht near Kos and came ashore[4] for dinner. There was the usual scrum[5] of paparazzi[6] and he got angry."

"To cut a long story short[7]," interrupts Susie. "Dawson threw a wine bottle at one of the photographers[8], but it hit and injured[9] a local policeman. And now he's in jail[10]."

"The press[11] are going to go crazy," says Nat.

---

1 current [ˋkɝənt] (a.) 當前的
2 feature [ˋfitʃɚ] (v.) 特載
3 tabloid [ˋtæblɔɪd] (n.)（以轟動性 報導為特點的）小報

4 ashore [əˋʃor] (adv.) 上岸
5 scrum [skrʌm] (n.) 並列爭球
6 paparazzi [ˌpɑpəˋrɑtsɪ] (n.) 狗仔隊 （paparazzo 的複數）

"Exactly," agrees John. "So we've had to offer Mrs Dawson sanctuary[12] here at the embassy. It seems to be the only place in Greece where we can guarantee[13] she will be safe from the photographers."

"So," continues Susie. "John and I have been talking." She turns to me. "We think that if she's here, it's better if you aren't here, Jake."

This is it. And here was me thinking they liked me. All those silly dreams about me and Dad being here together. They can't wait to get rid of me. I'm wondering where I'll go. Maybe one of my teachers will take me in until they contact Mum. And I feel really miserable[14] . . . so I almost miss the end of Susie's sentence.

"So, you and Nat and I will take the boat to Heraklion this evening and stay there. You'll probably enjoy it more anyway. Our house is only a few steps from the beach . . ."

I blink[15]. They're not sending me home. I'm going with them to . . . to where?

"Heraklion?" I ask.

"Yes," says Susie. "Crete. Our house is in Panormou. It's only about twenty minutes along the coast from Heraklion. There is no way I can work here with the English press on our doorstep."

Nat smiles. "Mum has a kiln[16] in Crete. She's always looking for excuses to get out of Athens, so she can work in her studio[17] there," she tells me quietly.

---

7 to cut a long story short 長話短說
8 photographer [fə`tɑgrəfə] (n.) 攝影師
9 injure [`ɪndʒə] (v.) 傷害
10 jail [dʒel] (n.) 監獄
11 press [prɛs] (n.) 新聞界
12 sanctuary [`sæŋktʃu͵ɛrɪ] (n.) 庇護所
13 guarantee [͵gærən`ti] (v.) 擔保
14 miserable [`mɪzərəbl̩] (a.) 悽慘的
15 blink [blɪŋk] (v.) 眨眼
16 kiln [kɪln] (n.) 窯
17 studio [`stjudɪ͵o] (n.) 工作室

Crete, I'm thinking. This is the island where Dad works. Maybe we can find out what he's been working on. Maybe he went back to Crete. Maybe we'll find him. And even though I'm really excited that I'm going to Crete, I also feel sad that Dad isn't here. It's just like being ten again and missing him when I play football for the school or have a part in the play.

I ought to[1] feel happy but I can't because I miss Dad so much. And it's so stupid, here I am at sixteen—well, almost sixteen—and I feel just the same.

Days go by[2] and there is no news about Dad. I'm sure that he just changed his mind about wanting to see me. I think Susie thinks the same. Only Nat is still certain that something has happened to him. So to please Nat I go on trying to find a way into Dad's laptop. I think we've tried every place in Greece. We just can't find his password.

Vicki at the British School rings one morning and tells us that Dad was working near Matala. It seems that a colleague has been away and that's why it's taken so long to get back to us.

Nat looks it up on a map. "You'll love Matala," she tells me. "Mum used to[3] go there in the Sixties. There are all these amazing caves where the hippies[4] lived. It was a center of love and peace and all that. Joni Mitchell wrote a song about it."

I smile. Sometimes Nat sounds very much like her mother.

"That's where she met Alex," she continues.

"Who?" I ask. "Joni Mitchell?"

"No," says Nat. "Mum. Didn't you know? She used to go out with[5] Alex."

"With Dad?"

The news, while astonishing[6], makes many things understandable. Like why my mother hated Greece. Like why I never stayed on Crete with John and Susie. Mum always hated anyone who knew Dad before her. It was as if she had to be the only thing in Dad's life.

"Yeah," says Nat. "It was years ago. Long before he met your mum. But they've stayed good friends. He stayed here after your mum threw him out."

Dad and Susie.

"Do you want to go to Matala?" I ask.

"Yeah. Why not?" says Nat. "We can camp[7] on the Red Beach. Mum won't mind. We might find out something."

I open Dad's laptop. One final try I think. Nat watches me.

"What about your name?" she suggests.

"What about it?" I say.

"Try it," she says.

"It's too short," I tell her.

"Then add your birthday," she says.

I type in "Jake1304", which is my birthday—13th April. And that's it.

1 ought to 應該
2 go by (時間) 流逝
3 used to 以前常常……
4 hippy ['hɪpɪ] (n.) 嬉皮
5 go out with 和某人約會
6 astonishing [ə'stɑnɪʃɪŋ] (a.) 令人吃驚的
7 camp [kæmp] (v.) 露營

I stare[1] at the screen in amazement as the icons[2] begin to pop up[3]. All this time away from me and Dad still uses my name and birthday. As if it really matters[4] to him. I don't want Nat to see how I feel.

"Let's go into Word and see what files pop up," says Nat.

I click the W icon. There is just one file in the recent history; it's called Melissa. Nat leans over me. Her hair presses[5] against my cheek; it smells of apples.

"Melissa?" says Nat. "That's a girl's name, isn't it?"

Melissa. So my first thoughts had been right. Dad had a new girlfriend, someone more interesting than a teenage son. All that stuff about black cars that Nat and I had discovered was just a fantasy. We were like children who read detective stories[6] and think that any stranger is an international jewel[7] thief. The car was probably some embassy car and the man wanted some information. Dad changed his mind and went off to see his girlfriend at the school. I was an idiot. I feel my whole mood change as if a black dog has climbed on my back.

I open the file. There is a small map and some letters and numbers.

"Melissa," says Nat, looking at the map. "It's a place near Matala."

A place. The black dog jumps off and disappears.

---

1 stare [stɛr] (v.) 盯；凝視
2 icon [ˈaɪkɑn] (n.)〔電腦〕軟體圖示
3 pop up 彈出來
4 matter [ˈmætɚ] (v.) 要緊
5 press [prɛs] (v.) 壓
6 detective story 偵探故事
7 jewel [ˈdʒuəl] (n.) 寶石

Moods

- What things put you into a good mood?
  What things put you into a bad mood?
- Jake says that his bad mood feels "as if a black dog climbed on his back". Think of a time you were in a bad mood. How would you describe it?
- Think of a time you were in a good mood. How would you describe it?

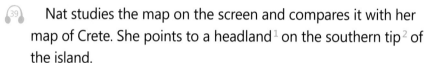

Nat studies the map on the screen and compares it with her map of Crete. She points to a headland[1] on the southern tip[2] of the island.

"It's as far south as you can get," she says. "After that, there's nothing between you and Africa."

"What are all those letters and numbers?" she asks.

"I think they're compass[3] readings," I say.

"Of course," she says. "Dad uses them when he goes sailing. How do you know?"

"I do lots of walking and climbing. We live beside the Dales at home." I tell her.

"Really?" she asks.

"Yes," I say. I knew she had no idea where I lived. "It looks as if there are very steep[4] cliffs[5]," I add, looking at the map.

---

1 headland [ˈhɛdlənd] (n.) 海角；岬
2 tip [tɪp] (n.) 尖端
3 compass [ˈkʌmpəs] (n.) 羅盤；指南針
4 steep [stip] (a.) 陡峭的
5 cliff [klɪf] (n.) 懸崖；峭壁
6 muppet [ˈmʌpɪt] (n.) 笨蛋

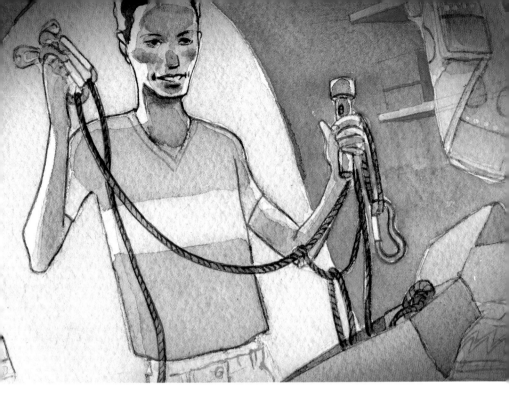

"Yeah," says Nat. "That's why there are caves, muppet[6]!"

"Muppet!" I retort[7]. "And who didn't recognize the compass readings?"

Nat punches[8] my shoulder in a sisterly kind of way and I think: I've never had a sister, but I've often wanted one. And Nat would be the best kind of sister.

The house in Panormou is exactly the kind of house you want to stay in. In every room you find interesting things from a previous holiday. There are piles of faded[9] beach towels and books with ruffled[10] pages that look as if they've fallen into the sea.

---

7 retort [rɪˈtɔrt] (v.) 反駁；回嘴   9 faded [ˈfedɪd] (a.) 褪色的
8 punch [pʌntʃ] (v.) 用拳猛擊   10 ruffled [ˈrʌfld] (a.) 弄縐的

In one corner I find some climbing equipment[1] that someone once left behind. Nat's never climbed so we can't do any clever stuff, but I always like to be prepared, so I lift[2] some ropes, and a compass, as well as making sure we've got torches[3] and spare[4] batteries.

Nat laughs and calls me a boy scout[5], but I've helped rescue[6] people in the Dales who forgot to take any proper equipment.

The next day we leave early for Melissa. Crete is not what I expected. It's not like other islands. It's bigger, for one thing and it keeps changing. The house in Panormou is on a cliff above a tiny bay where the sea is deep green, but in other places there are just long beaches and the sea is an incredibly deep blue.

As we drive south, it changes. There are little villages and deep ravines[7] with racing[8] streams[9] that remind me of home and, then miles of rocky mountainside that looks like the surface of the moon.

---

1 equipment [ɪ`kwɪpmənt] (n.) 配備　　3 torch [tɔrtʃ] (n.) 火炬；火把
2 lift [lɪft] (v.) 舉起；拿起　　　　 4 spare [spɛr] (a.) 備用的

We're driving through a valley of grapevines and olive trees and a scattering[10] of old rundown[11] houses when I see a familiar face. He is sitting outside a café talking to two men. I turn away, but I think I'm too late. He's seen me.

"What?" asks Nat.

"That was Nikos. The police inspector I met in Athens," I say.

"What's he doing here?" she asks.

"I don't know. Do you think he knows where Dad is?"

"I don't know," she says. "But it proves[12] I'm right. Something is going on."

We've decided to try and follow Dad's compass readings. Using one of John's sailing maps we think they correspond to somewhere east of Melissa, between Matala and a tiny place called Kali Limenes. The problem is that there isn't a road and we don't have a boat.

5 scout [skaut] (n.) 童子軍
6 rescue [ˈrɛskju] (v.) 營救
7 ravine [rəˈvin] (n.) 深谷
8 racing [ˈresɪŋ] (a.) 奔流的

9 stream [strim] (n.) 小河
10 scattering [ˈskætərɪŋ] (n.) 分散；散落
11 rundown [ˈrʌnˌdaun] (a.) 失修的；破敗的
12 prove [pruv] (v.) 證明

"We can leave the car at Kali Limenes," says Nat. "Then we can walk."

"There seems to be a path[1] here," I point to the map. "It goes up to a monastery[2] and there's another small path that leads back to the sea, towards Melissa."

In fact we find a fairly[3] new track[4] which we follow for a bit and then we leave it and take the small path. It's not easy walking. There are lots of small stones and fierce[5] thorn bushes, but we follow what looks like a goat path along a ridge[6] and find ourselves in a clearing[7]. The path stops and the sea is below us.

"Someone's been here," says Nat.

"But why would someone come here?" I ask. "There's nothing here!"

We take off our backpacks[8] to drink some water and my water bottle rolls away towards a big thorn bush. I leap after it and there it is. It's behind the bush. The entrance to a cave.

"So that's why he came here," says Nat.

"Dad?" I ask. "You think he was here?"

"Of course," she says. "He was exploring[9] the caves."

We go back for our backpacks and take out our torches and begin to explore the cave. It's quite small, though it does look as if someone has recently widened the opening. Inside it's narrow with several rock ledges[10].

---

1 path [pæθ] (n.) 小徑
2 monastery [ˋmɑnəsˌtɛrɪ] (n.) 僧院
3 fairly [ˋfɛrlɪ] (adv.) 相當地
4 track [træk] (n.) 小道
5 fierce [fɪrs] (a.) 尖銳的
6 ridge [rɪdʒ] (n.) 山脊
7 clearing [ˋklɪrɪŋ] (n.) 林中的空地
8 backpack [ˋbækˌpæk] (n.) 登山背包
9 explore [ɪkˋsplor] (v.) 探索
10 ledge [lɛdʒ] (n.) 岩石突出的部分

"It's not just one cave," says Nat.

"No," I agree. "There's a whole cave system here with tunnels[1]. We need to mark the walls so we can find our way back."

"I don't like it," says Nat. "And it's freezing[2]."

The Cave

- Would you have gone into the cave? Why/why not?
- Which of these adjectives best describes Jake and Nat's decision to go into the cave? Explain why.

  brave   foolish   reckless[3]   wise

"Look!" I say. "I can see light. We've found another way out."

"Thank goodness," says Nat, as we stumble[4] through the tunnel and out into the light.

We've come right through the mountain on to the other side. We're back in the valley and bang in the middle of[5] a farm. It looks very rundown except for a couple of sheds[6] made of corrugated[7] iron which look new. They also have large padlocks[8] on them which look extremely[9] new. Too new.

---

1 tunnel [ˈtʌnl]] (n.) 隧道
2 freezing [ˈfrizɪŋ] (a.) 極冷的
3 reckless [ˈrɛklɪs] (a.) 魯莽的
4 stumble [ˈstʌmbl] (v.) 絆倒
5 bang in the middle of 在正中間
6 shed [ʃɛd] (n.) 棚；小屋
7 corrugated [ˈkɔrəˌgetɪd] (a.) 成波狀的

8 padlock [ˈpædˌlɑk] (n.) 掛鎖
9 extremely [ɪkˈstrimlɪ] (adv.) 極度地
10 bang [bæŋ] (v.) 猛擊
11 kidnapper [ˈkɪdnæpɚ] (n.) 綁票者
12 grab [græb] (v.) 攫取
13 gunpoint [ˈgʌnˌpɔɪnt] (n.) 槍口
14 despite [dɪˈspaɪt] (prep.) 儘管

Then everything happens very fast.

Nat calls: "Jake!" but I'm not listening to her.

I am suddenly certain that I've found Dad. And I run. And I shout. I run up to one of the sheds and bang[10] on the walls and shout: "Dad! Dad! It's me! It's Jake!"

This is probably the most stupid thing I have ever done. I mean, how do you let a kidnapper[11] know that you have discovered him? The answer is: shout and make a lot of noise.

It takes the men about one minute to run out of the house. It takes them another minute for them to grab[12] Nat and me at gunpoint[13] and push us indoors. They are not pleased to see us.

They hit me in the face so hard that I fall over and then they hold a gun at Nat's head. Then they say they're going to kill her unless I tell them everything. So I tell them everything. Well, almost everything. I don't say she's the daughter of the British Ambassador. For some reason, I say she's my sister. And despite[14] being terrified, I see Nat give a small smile.

The men seem to believe me and move away to talk. There are five of them, two of them, who seem to be in charge[1], are talking a language I don't understand. The other three I think are North African. Their only common language seems to be English, but it's hard to understand them. I hear phrases[2] which include the words "wait" and "late" and the name "Bamir". I also hear "archaeologist" and I'm certain they're talking about Dad. I'm beginning to think they've killed him. I feel sick.

Nat reaches across the floor towards me and squeezes[3] my hand. I try to smile, but my jaw[4] is really painful. I wonder if I can get to my phone, but one of the men has thought of that. He grabs our backpacks and our phones.

But it seems they don't have time to deal with[5] us right now. They tie our hands and feet and push us into a back room. There's something really horrible going on and I'm so scared[6] I can hardly think. Luckily Nat's brain is still working.

"We've got to get out of here," whispers Nat. "It's just too dangerous. Can you move at all?"

Danger

- What would you do if you were in this situation?
- Have you ever been in a dangerous situation?
  What happened? What did you do?

I edge[7] myself towards her and try to undo[8] the ropes round her wrists with my teeth. In the movies it looks really easy, but it's actually really hard. Gradually, I manage to loosen the first knot[9] and work it free[10]. The next knot is easier and after what seems like ages, I manage to get the ropes off Nat's hands.

She quickly undoes the ropes round her ankles and then undoes my ropes. There is a small window in the room which faces the mountain side of the farm. It squeaks as we open it and we stop, expecting one of the men to come rushing in.

1 in charge 負責
2 phrase [frez] (n.) 詞組
3 squeeze [skwiz] (v.) 擠；緊握
4 jaw [dʒɔ] (n.) 下巴
5 deal with 處理

6 scared [skɛrd] (a.) 嚇壞的
7 edge [ɛdʒ] (v.) 側著移動
8 undo [ʌnˋdu] (v.) 解開
9 knot [nɑt] (n.) 結
10 work it free 打開；解開

But as we open the window we hear a terrible noise. A woman is screaming[1]. It's coming from the sheds.

"What have we walked into?" whispers Nat, echoing my thoughts. Who is the woman? And where's Dad?

We know we can't go back near the sheds or the front of the farm, so the only way is upwards. We ease[2] ourselves out of the window and I jump first. Nat follows me, but her ankle goes over and she falls.

I help her up, but she's very white and I'm worried sick that she's broken something.

"Can you move your foot?" I ask

She nods. "I think it's just a sprain[3]," she says. "It's my ankle."

The men are all busy in the sheds so they don't see us as we crawl[4] away between the thorn bushes and up the hillside. We reach the edge at the top and realize why the men didn't need to fence[5] the top of the farm. It's a sheer[6] drop down the other side, about thirty meters before some fairly flat rocks. Then there's another drop down to the sea. And the men have our ropes.

"We have to go back the other way," says Nat.

I begin to study the cliff. It's not as sheer as I first thought. It is climbable.

"We can't." I say. "They'll kill us. We have to go down."

"But I don't think I can stand," Nat begins.

"I'll carry you," I say. "Don't worry. It's not a hard climb. I can do it."

1 scream [skrim] (v.) 尖叫
2 ease [iz] (v.) 小心地移置
3 sprain [spren] (v.) 扭傷
4 crawl [krɔl] (v.) 爬行；緩慢移動
5 fence [fɛns] (v.) 設置籬笆
6 sheer [ʃɪr] (a.) 陡峭的
7 flatten [ˈflætn̩] (v.) 使平坦
8 whisper [ˈhwɪspɚ] (v.) 低聲說
9 foothold [ˈfʊtˌhold] (n.) 踏腳處

I feel really sick as I say this. I've never done a climb like this on my own or without a rope. But there isn't any choice. I sit down so Nat can get onto my back.

"I've had packs heavier than you," I say as I stand up. "I need you to flatten[7] yourself into my back as much as you can."

"OK", Nat whispers[8] into my neck.

"And don't look down," I add.

"I can't," she says.

I begin to edge down. One foothold[9], one handhold[10] at a time. I've never climbed down a rock face like this without proper equipment, but it's not impossible. You just have to know how to grasp[11] each hold[12]. If you do it wrong, you fall.

"Don't think," I say to myself. "Just concentrate[13] on the holds. One by one."

The rock is dry and hard. It doesn't crumble[14]; it isn't slippery[15]. "Just do it," I say to myself. "You can do it."

Step by step, with every hold sending waves of pain through my arms, I climb down the cliff. It seems as if hours are passing, but finally I can feel the flat rock under my feet. I start breathing again. I've done it.

"We're safe," I say.

Nat begins to cry and I hug her so she doesn't see that I'm crying, too.

After a bit we try to think what to do next. Below us the rock is much steeper and falls straight into the sea. It's not a climb I can do without ropes and certainly not with Nat on my back.

---

10 handhold ['hænd,hold] (n.) 手可以抓的地方
11 grasp [græsp] (v.) 抓牢
12 hold [hold] (n.) 可手攀或腳踏之處
13 concentrate ['kɑnsɛn,tret] (v.) 集中
14 crumble ['krʌmbl] (v.) 碎裂
15 slippery ['slɪpərɪ] (a.) 滑的

"Perhaps a boat will come by and see us," she says. "Mum will start looking for us when I don't phone. They'll send a helicopter[1]."

Then we hear it. It's on the other side of the mountain, and faint. But we know what it is.

"Gunfire[2]?" I ask.

I think of the woman who was screaming and Dad and I go cold all over[3]. After a bit the shooting[4] stops and all we can hear is the sea and the wind.

"It looks as if there are some more caves here," I say. "I'll go and look in case[5] we need somewhere to shelter[6] overnight."

The entrance again looks as if someone has opened it. And just inside I discover a miraculous[7] store[8]. Bottles of water, a torch, paper and some matches[9].

I almost run back to Nat with the water. She insists on coming with me to look and I support her as she limps[10] over.

"Someone's been working here," she says.

"Do you think it's the men?" I ask.

She shakes her head. "They don't look like climbers. I think it's Alex."

I take the torch and together we make our way inside. Then we see them. They are all along the walls. Paintings of animals and men. Men with spears[11] and men with what looks like stones. Just like the caves at Lascaux[12]. Incredible and so bright. Like red fire.

---

1 helicopter [ˈhɛlɪˌkɑptɚ] (n.) 直升機
2 gunfire [ˈgʌnˌfaɪr] (n.) 槍戰
3 go cold all over 全身發冷
4 shooting [ˈʃutɪŋ] (n.) 射擊
5 in case 假使
6 shelter [ˈʃɛltɚ] (v.) 找庇身之處
7 miraculous [mɪˈrækjələs] (a.) 神奇的

8 store [stor] (n.) 儲藏品
9 match [mætʃ] (n.) 火柴
10 limp [lɪmp] (v.) 一瘸一拐地走
11 spear [spɪr] (n.) 矛；魚叉
12 Lascaux [lɑˈsko] 法國拉斯科洞窟
   （著名的石器時代洞穴壁畫）

"This is what Dad found," I say.

"Which means he also found the farm," says Nat. "Which means . . ."

She doesn't finish the sentence. We're both thinking about the gunfire and trying not to cry.

Then I hear something.

"There's someone coming," I say.

We look around. This is it. There's nowhere left to hide. We can't go up or down.

"Jake," says Nat. She takes my hand. "I just want to say . . ."

Last words

- What do you think Nat wants to say to Jake? Write then share with a partner.

But I never find out what she wants to say because I suddenly hear someone calling her name. And mine.

"Alex?" whispers Nat.

"Dad?" I whisper.

Then we shout: "Alex! Dad! We're here!"

And the man I've wanted to see for so many years is there in front of me and he's hugging us and crying and we're crying and hugging him back.

He carries Nat back outside so we can sit and talk.

"We need to wait a bit for the police to clear up[1] before we go back through the cave," he says.

"It leads to the farm, too?" I ask.

Dad nods. "I found this out a few weeks ago. I've been working here for several months, but I only found this cave a few weeks back. I couldn't believe it. It changes everything. We didn't know there were people living here so long ago."

"And the farm . . .?" asks Nat.

"What is it?" I ask.

"It's used for people smuggling," says Dad. "They bring illegal[2] immigrants[3] in by boat and through the caves to the farm. There's another cave at sea level[4] they use."

"But why haven't the police arrested[5] them?" asks Nat.

"They have now," says Dad. "Didn't you hear the gunfire?"

"That was the police?" I ask.

"Yes," says Dad. "They've been waiting for the boss. They wanted to catch the top man." He turns to me. "Jake, I'm so sorry. It's been a terrible mess[6]. I thought I was doing the right thing and I can see now I did everything wrong."

"But why?" I ask. "Why didn't you tell me?"

"The police told me to keep away from the caves," says Dad. "I thought the smugglers hadn't noticed me but on my way to the airport I discovered that they were following me."

 "The man in the black car," says Nat.

"I panicked[7]," says Dad. "I didn't want them to know about you. They are incredibly violent[8]," he adds. "I wanted you to go back home."

"But didn't Inspector Nikos tell you I couldn't go home?" I asked.

"No," says Dad, grimly[9]. "He didn't. Not until today. He saw you drive through Pompia and guessed you were coming here. So he called me and I came straight here. And just in time . . ."

*   *   *   *   *   *

After a bit, Dad's phone goes and he says it's safe.

He carries Nat through the cave and back to the farm which is full of police cars.

And Nat goes to the hospital and it is just a sprain and Alex comes home and we tell Susie and John the story again and again. And they're amazing about it and tell me how brave I am and they aren't angry.

---

1 clear up 清理
2 illegal [ɪˈligl] (a.) 非法的
3 immigrant [ˈɪməgrənt] (n.) 移民
4 seal level 海平線
5 arrest [əˈrɛst] (v.) 逮捕
6 mess [mɛs] (n.) 混亂
7 panic [ˈpænɪk] (v.) 恐慌（動詞三態： panic; panicked; panicked）
8 violent [ˈvaɪələnt] (a.) 兇暴的
9 grimly [ˈgrɪmlɪ] (adv.) 嚴肅地

(54) We're sitting on the terrace[1] in Panormou drinking coffee and talking about future holidays and suddenly I realize they are including me. They want me and Dad to stay with them again in Crete.

And we're all laughing and talking when we hear a shot. And Inspector Nikos appears.

"I am sorry," he says. "There was one man we didn't capture[2] yesterday. He was following you."

"But you've got him now?" asks Susie, white as a sheet[3].

"Yes," says Nikos. "Now you are safe. He is the last man. Now you can really enjoy your holidays."

And we do. Dad takes us back to the caves to see the earth paintings one final time before they are photographed and closed behind glass to protect them from the public[4]. And he gives me the small piece of red earth painted seventeen thousand years ago. But I don't need it. I've got Dad.

1 terrace ['tɛrəs] (n.) 露臺
2 capture ['kæptʃɚ] (v.) 捕獲
3 sheet [ʃit] (n.) 床單
4 the public 社會大眾

AFTER READING

Ⓐ Personal Response

1 Did you enjoy the story? Why/why not?

2 Do you think that the title *Danger in the Sun,* is suitable? With a partner think of another two possible titles.

3 Would you have done the same things as Jake did? What would you have done differently?

4 Did the story remind you of any other stories you have read or films you have seen? Tell the rest of the class about them.

5 Imagine you are making a film of the story. Design a poster for the film. Choose a song for the start of the film.

B Characters

6 Answer the questions about Jake.

- a) How old is Jake?
- b) Who does Jake live with?
- c) What is Jake's mother doing while he is in Greece?
- d) What is one of Jake's hobbies?
- e) How does Jake feel about his father?
- f) Why does Jake like being with Nat's family?

7 Who is Jake talking about? Write their names.

- a) S/he is younger than the other policeman and looks more efficient.
- b) S/he has got a kind educated voice.
- c) S/he's so friendly. I feel as if I've always known him/her.
- d) I know that whatever else happens in my life, I want … as a friend.
- e) It's just like being ten again and missing him/her when I play football for the school.
- f) S/he always hated anyone who knew Dad before him/her.

8 Which adjectives describe Nat Parsons? Tick them.

☐ violent   ☐ resourceful
☐ talkative   ☐ friendly
☐ absent-minded   ☐ snobby
☐ kind   ☐ thoughtful
☐ creative   ☐ slow

9 Answer the following questions.

   a What did Jake think Nat was going to be like?
   b Why did he think this?
   c Why did he change his mind?

10 Read the sentences about Alexander Wyatt, Jake's father.
Then tick True (T) or False (F).

   T F   a Jake's father is an architect.
   T F   b He left home when Jake was ten years old.
   T F   c He had an affair with a young archaeologist.
   T F   d He has never written to Jake on his birthday or at Christmas.
   T F   e His brother died when he was seven.
   T F   f He is selfish and mean. He never thinks about other people.
   T F   g He used to be married to Nat's mum.
   T F   h Jake's name and age is the password on his laptop.
   T F   i He has got a girlfriend called Melissa.

C Plot

11 Jake's father doesn't come to the airport to meet him. Why not?
Match the characters below to their comments on Jake's father.

[1] Jake's mother   [2] the ambassador, John Parsons
[3] Nikos Filopapos   [4] the girl at airport information
[5] the hotel receptionist   [6] the tourist police
[7] Susie Parsons

     [a] The traffic's terrible. He must be delayed.
     [b] This isn't like Alex at all.
     [c] He left three hours ago because he didn't want
         to be late.
     [d] Perhaps he forgot.
     [e] You can't rely on him.
     [f] You should go home until we find him.
     [g] It's probably some work thing.

12 Work with a partner. A is
a police officer with the
tourist police and B is Jake.
Ask and answer questions
about Jake's father.

13 What is the main plot of the story. What are the sub plots?
Choose from below. Describe how each of the plots develops.

[a] Jake's friendship with Nat
[b] Jake's search for his father
[c] The smugglers
[d] The discovery of the cave paintings

14 Answer the questions.

a) Why did Jake and his mother have a row?

b) What did Jake find in the hotel room?

c) What did Inspector Nikos want Jake to do?

d) Where did Nat and Jake find Alex's laptop?

e) Why did Jake have to leave the embassy and go to Crete?

f) What or who is Melissa?

g) What are the letters and numbers on the map on Alex's laptop?

h) Where did the cave lead to?

i) How did the kidnappers find Jake and Nat?

j) What did the kidnappers do with Jake and Nat?

k) Why couldn't Nat climb down the cliff?

15 This is Alex's account of events. Then match the green words to the definitions.

I found this (a) cave a few weeks ago. It leads to the farm They use the farm for people (b) smuggling. They bring illegal (c) immigrants here by boat. The police didn't (d) arrest them before because they were waiting for the (e) top man. The police told me to keep away. I didn't think the smugglers had noticed me. Then on the way to the airport I (f) noticed they were following me. I didn't come to meet you because I (g) panicked. The smugglers are very (h) violent so I wanted you to go back home.

_____ 1 boss
_____ 2 fierce and aggressive
_____ 3 a hole in the side of a cliff or hill
_____ 4 take someone and question them about a crime
_____ 5 people who go to live in another country
_____ 6 taking something or somebody illegally from one country to another
_____ 7 suddenly felt afraid or worried
_____ 8 saw

16 Every year, hundreds of people die trying to get to Europe. There are lots of articles about people smuggling on the Internet. Find one of these stories. Then tell the class about it.

❶ Language

17 Complete the dialogues with the expressions below.

1. Yes, that's what's bothering me.
2. I won't feel happy until it's all sorted out.
3. He's just getting back at you. You said some terrible stuff, too.
4. No, thanks. I'm not in the mood.
5. I'm just going to pop across to Sam's.
6. I've just had a row with my mum.

a
A Would you like to come to the cinema with us?
B

b
A What's the matter, Emma?
B

c
A Where are you going, Jake? It's nearly dinner time.
B   I won't be long.

d
A He said some horrible things.
B

e
A You don't look very happy.
B

f
A It says here that you have to be a good swimmer.
B   I can't swim!

18 Complete the sentences with had to or didn't have to.

[a] Jake _____ go to the hotel by himself.

[b] Jake _____ go back home to England.

[c] Jake _____ dress up while he stayed at the embassy.

[d] Jake _____ leave the embassy when the footballer's wife came to stay.

[e] Nat and Jake _____ find the password before they could look on Alex's laptop.

[f] Nat _____ climb down the cliff. Jake carried her.

19 What did the characters want or not want Jake to do? Complete the sentences.

- look for his father
- go back home
- spend the summer holidays with him
- see his father

[a] Jake's father

[b] Jake's mum

[c] Inspector Nikos

[d] Nat

20 Complete the sentences with the present or past passive form of the verbs in brackets.

a) Jake's father's letters _____ (send back) to him unread.

b) Venus from Milos and the great Marbles _____ (take) to London by Lord Elgin.

c) "You can stay at the embassy until everything _____ (sort out)," says Susie.

d) Nat thinks that the embassy _____ (haunt).

e) Nat and Jake _____ (tie up) by the smugglers.

VENUS FROM MILOS

87

TEST

1 Tick True (T) or False (F).

T F ⓐ Jake has visited the Parthenon a thousand times.

T F ⓑ Jake has not seen his father for five years.

T F ⓒ Jake discovered a letter from his father on his birthday.

T F ⓓ Jake's uncle lives in Canada.

T **F** (e) Nat's mother is an archaeologist too.

T **F** (f) Nat doesn't phone the hotel on the embassy phone because she thinks it's bugged.

T **F** (g) Jake's mum is an Art teacher.

T **F** (h) Nat's mum used to go out with Jake's dad.

T **F** (i) Jake thinks that Melissa is the name of a place but it is in fact the name of his dad's new girlfriend.

T **F** (j) Jake likes climbing but Nat has never climbed before.

T **F** (k) Jake sees Inspector Nikos sitting outside a café on the island of Crete.

T **F** (l) Nat drops her water bottle and finds the entrance to a cave.

T **F** (m) Nat and Jake walk through a tunnel in the mountainside and come out in the middle of a farm.

T **F** (n) Jake manages to untie the knots and free Nat's hands.

T **F** (o) Jake finally meets his father in the cave with the animal paintings on the walls.

2 With a partner correct the false sentences.

3 You have just read the story of Jake's summer holiday. Write an email to Jake and tell him about the best summer holiday you have ever had. These questions will help you.

★ Where did you go?
★ What did you do there?
★ Who did you go with?
★ Why was it special?

4 Listen to the conversation between Jake and Nikos. Then tick True (T) or False (F).

T **F** (a) Jake knows what his father is working on at the moment.

T **F** (b) They need archaeology police in Greece because there are a lot of treasures to steal.

T **F** (c) Nikos is sure that Jake's father has stolen something valuable.

T **F** (d) Jake's father has an office in Crete and one at the British School in Athens.

T **F** (e) Jake hasn't looked through his father's belongings at all.

T **F** (f) Jake found a small piece of rock amongst his father's belongings.

T **F** (g) Nikos wants to have the paint on the rock analyzed.

T **F** (h) Jake's father may be trying to smuggle something out of Greece. Nikos is not sure.

5 Talk about the pictures.

a Look at the picture on page 19.
Partner A tell Partner B about the picture.

Who is in the picture?
Where is s/he? Describe the place.
What is s/he doing?

b Then look at the picture on page 71.
Partner B tell Partner A
about the picture.

Who is in the picture?
How do they look?
Where are they?

1 Skim the text and match the numbers to the questions.

150   4,000   11,000

[a] What is the population of Agathonisi?

[b] How many illegal immigrants have arrived in Greece this year?

[c] How many immigrants have already arrived on the island of Agathonisi?

People Smuggling

This year, groups of men, women and children from as far away as Afghanistan and Iraq began arriving on the small Greek island of Agathonisi. The island has a population of 150 people. It can't cope with the large numbers of immigrants that are arriving. More than 4,000 immigrants have already arrived on the island. They are ferried by smugglers to Agathonisi from nearby Turkey.

"We're a warm-hearted people and at first we welcomed them with open arms," said Evangelos Kottoros, the head of the tiny community. "We gave them food. And we gave them clothes but we haven't got the facilities to look after them. On some days nearly 200 people arrived. They are all desperate to flee poverty and conflict." After around 700 immigrants climbed out of little old boats onto Agathonisi's shores in the space of ten days, local authorities made an urgent appeal for help. Every day now immigrants illegally enter Greece. The government estimates that more than 11,000 have arrived this year. Most slip in along the country's craggy coastline.

2 Find some statistics about people smuggling to your country or another country in Europe on the Internet. Tell the class the results of your search.

3 Why do people leave their countries? In pairs, make a list of reasons. Then discuss as a class.

作者簡介

請問你是在什麼時候知道自己想要走上寫作這條路的？

其實我倒想說我記不起來什麼時候想要封筆過。我最早的作品是一齣戲劇，那是我和家人在聖誕節表演的戲碼，我當時八歲。即使在從事其他事情時，我始終知道自己是作家。除了能夠坐下來寫東西，其他的事情都像是在打發時間。

你提到戲劇，你目前還有在寫劇本嗎？抑或只是寫小說？

我寫了很多英語讀本的故事，也會寫劇本，因為我喜歡這種挑戰，能夠透過劇中人物的語言行為來呈現人物的性格。這和寫小說很不一樣，而當你目睹到演員們正在飾演你所創造出來的角色時，是非常令人興奮的。

你會如何開始一部小說的寫作？

我不會坐著等靈感上門。我常常會找一個議題來下手，例如會讓我感到憤怒或憂慮的事情。接著，我會開始設計角色，誰會與這個議題關係密切？什麼樣的人又會受到影響或是被牽連進去？

為什麼你會寫這篇小說？

我通常是以「假設性問題」的情境展開小說創作的，比方說假如在飛抵某個機場後，發現原本要接機的人沒有出現的話，你會怎麼辦？這篇故事就是從這裡開始的。接著我得認識傑可這個人，想想他是什麼樣的人？他想要的又是什麼？這篇故事的重點在於角色的鋪陳，而非故事情節。

你去過希臘嗎？

我在雅典住過四年，我那時候常常去克里特島，那是一個很棒的島嶼。這個故事裡所提到的很多地方我都知道，那些地方充滿了戲劇張力。你可以想像發生在那裡的事情。

P.15

　　以下是我的遐想：我和爸爸正在雅典，在雅典的哪裡呢？大概是在帕德嫩神殿，沒錯，我和爸爸就站在衛城的中央。好吧，我也知道這裡正在修葺，不准閒雜人等進入，但這只是我的想像，好嗎？總之我來到了這裡，雖然我在海報或明信片上看過衛城上千遍了，但想像中的衛城還是很不一樣。

　　是同一個地方沒錯，但感覺並不完全一樣。我很喜歡這個地方，這裡古意盎然，突然之間，我明白了爸爸為什麼當考古學家了。

　　這時爸爸對著我看了看，看著我所有的表情。我看得出來，他這一刻是無比滿足的，而且我也知道這就是他一直渴望的事──和兒子一起分享他對希臘的熱愛。

　　「我猜你來這裡已經幾百次了。」我說。

　　「大概有幾十次吧。」他回答道：「以前，在週日和滿月的晚上可以自由進出，我們常會帶瓶葡萄酒上來，為古希臘的光輝燦爛乾杯。」

　　「那是古時候的事了。」我開玩笑道。

　　「是啊，那時候恐龍還橫行於地球。」他說。

　　這是我們父子之間的笑話。我們有不少笑話，有許多事也是一起攜手做的。

　　我對爸爸亞歷克斯‧懷特有很多的想像，以上是其中的一個想像。

P.16

　　我已經有五年沒見到爸爸了，他上一次離家時我才十歲。此刻，我來到了雅典的機場，這一次我們父子終於可以在一起好好度個假了。我們會去衛城，他會向我介紹令人嘆為觀止的東西，我們也會一起搞笑，除非……

　　除非我來到了雅典的機場，而他卻放我鴿子。他沒有來機場接我，我不知道是什麼原因。

等候

- 你想懷特先生為什麼沒有去接兒子？
- 你曾經枯等，結果對方遲到很久或是爽約嗎？你當時的心情如何？結果你怎麼處理？

　　我找出了他最近寄給我的一封電子郵件，信裡頭寫道：「很高興你終於要來了，下午兩點二十分，我會在機場接你。」

但現在已經下午三點半了，我站在那些舉著「瓊斯先生」、「奧林匹克飯店」等各種招牌的人群中。這時我決定，不要讓我的假期待在雅典機場裡和一大堆陌生人窮耗。我只想找到爸爸，但我的人生卻總是如此：在我需要他的時候，他都不在我身邊。我很生氣，厭煩透了這種情況。

P.17

在我十歲時，我很需要爸爸，我都會為他找藉口，但現在我已經不是十歲的小孩，沒有興致編織故事。我要親自去找爸爸，然後告訴他，他的獨子在闊別五年後來找他，而他卻放我鴿子。他需要一個很好的藉口，一個絕佳的理由。

接著我便展開行動。我先到服務台，一頭深色頭髮的美麗櫃台小姐微笑地對我說，很抱歉，我父親不在那裡。接著，她透過廣播，用嚴厲的語氣喊道：「亞歷克斯‧懷特先生，請立刻到服務台，您的兒子傑可正在這裡等您。」

過了好一會兒，爸爸仍然沒有現身，她看起來有些擔心，問我是否還好。我告訴她我沒事，我會去飯店等他。於是她又笑了笑，並說雅典的交通狀況很可怕，爸爸一定是受到了耽擱。

我換了些錢，按照好心的服務台小姐的指示，搭乘地鐵到憲法廣場站，那裡是議會的所在地，距離我的飯店只有兩分鐘的腳程。根據爸爸的講法，這家飯店最棒的地方，是可以從屋頂上看到衛城。當我抵達飯店時，發現爸爸的確為我們訂了一個房間，而且有和櫃台人員談到我會來，還說我終於要來雅典了，他太高興了。

「我想不透他為什麼沒去接機，他怕遲到，三個小時之前就出去了。」櫃台人員憂心地說。

P.18

櫃台人員把房間鑰匙給了我，於是我便先上樓。我推開門走進房間，看到裡面有一個小箱子和幾件衣服，這些東西想必是屬於那個被我稱作爸爸的人，但我不確定，我們已經有五年沒見面了。

我覺得我待在一個陌生人的房間裡，最讓我生氣的是，媽媽那番話言猶在耳：「你瞧瞧，傑可，我說得沒錯吧！你爸爸根本就不關心你，你不要再指望他了。」

我不想聽媽媽說這種話，我寧可相信爸爸很關心我，但沒想到卻發生了這種事情。我跟自己說，我先去屋頂的游泳池裡游個泳，爸爸等一下就會到了，然後我們再一起去衛城，我們會像一般的父子那樣互相打趣。

於是我先去游了一陣泳，從那裡眺望衛城，視野絕佳，就像明信片上看到的照片一樣，但又感覺不太一樣。然而，爸爸的人還是沒有出現。

我又打了他的手機（撥了又撥），手機一直沒開機。為什麼會這樣？這完全不合常理，我知道爸爸也很想見我，還是說，他是故意要用這種可怕的方法來報復媽媽？不，不可能，媽媽巴不得能證明爸爸是個很不可靠的人。

我現在之所以會在這裡，是因為在四

親愛的傑可：

　　生日快樂，十五歲了喲，我想你現在一定長得跟我差不多高了。不過在我的腦海裡，你還是那個穿著燈芯絨褲子的小男孩，那是我那麼多年以前最後見到你的樣子。我想你還是不想理我，就像你媽媽在信中說的那樣，不過一如往常，我還是會在你的生日和聖誕節時寫信給你，因為你是我的兒子，我那麼愛你，也很想你。希望有一天你會原諒我，我們父子可以再度聚首，到時候或許我可以帶你去希臘到處看一下，我們也可以重新認識彼此。但願你今年不會再原信退還。

年又十個月之後，我發現媽媽每次講的那種話都不是真的，她說：「你爸爸根本不把你當一回事！」

　　我是在我生日那天發現到這件事的，那天我起了個大早，所以先去拿郵件。

P. 20

　　當時父親的來信就靜靜地躺在客廳的地毯上，我現在坐在雅典市中心這家飯店裡讀的信，就是那封信。我看著衣櫃裡掛著的亞麻布夾克，心想：「這是爸爸的夾克，他穿亞麻布夾克。」

　　那封信──信的內容我倒背如流，因為我已經看了不知多少遍了──信上這樣寫道：

P. 21

　　因為這封信，我開始向媽媽大吼大叫。我問她這到底是怎麼一回事，她怎麼可以這樣？我們為了這件事激烈地爭吵了幾天。媽媽哭著說我不懂，我也說她不懂我。爸爸每年都寫信給我，而我卻被蒙在鼓裡，我到現在都還沒辦法原諒媽媽。

　　爸爸又不是罪犯，他是考古學家，和另一位年輕的女考古學家發生了婚外情，媽媽發現後就把他趕出家門，還跟他說，他永遠都別想再見到我了。我在他們的爭吵中成了一個棋子，好像把我當成是一個沒有感覺、沒有需求的人，好像在成長過程中認為父親對自己漠不關心也無所謂。但事實並非如此。

P. 22

祕密

・傑可的媽媽隱瞞了父親的信，你想她為什麼要這樣做？
・你曾經向別人隱瞞過什麼事嗎？為什麼你會這麼做？

　　在和媽媽爭吵過後，我打電話給爸爸，出乎意外地和他聊了很久。後來我們互相寫電子郵件，他邀請我暑假時去希臘找他。媽媽氣得幾乎不和我說話，她決定暑假時要去蘇格蘭的一個瑜珈會館，找回自己，起碼她是這樣說的。

　　最後，我終於來到了希臘，可是父親還是不在我身邊，而且我也不知道媽媽在哪裡。我想她沒有跟我提過那間瑜珈會館的名字，但我記得她說過那個地方與世無爭，甚至連電話都沒有。現在已經是晚上八點鐘左右，我還是不知道爸爸到底是怎麼一回事。

　　到了九點，櫃枱人員猜想爸爸可能是出了意外，於是打電話報警，請他們聯絡各個醫院。結果所有的醫院都沒有爸爸的消息，於是接待人員又猜想他可能是遇到了朋友，一起喝了酒。我爸爸是個酒鬼嗎？爸爸有提過這件事嗎？接待人員說這只是他個人的猜測，爸爸並沒有提到這件事。

P. 23

　　「你何不先去布拉卡區附近走一走，認識一下雅典？我想他明天早上就會出現了。」接待人員說。

　　於是我去布拉卡區逛了逛，看看那些古蹟，並吃了一塊從路邊攤買來的起司餅。觀光客們在葡萄藤下的小餐廳吃著晚餐，看起來很愜意，我討厭他們，也討厭爸爸。爸爸為什麼要這樣對我？

　　之後我回飯店睡覺，到了第二天早上，當然，爸爸還是沒有出現。接待人員於是建議我去找負責觀光的外事警察。

　　警察局裡出奇的吵雜，裡頭擠滿了鬼吼鬼叫或是哭哭啼啼的觀光客，他們遇到的問題不是丟了錢或護照、機票等等的，要不然就是外出閒逛卻忘了飯店的名稱。這些外事警察看起來超有耐心的。

「我這次度假要用的錢都在裡面！」排在我前面的婦人向警察說道，這種事警察是司空見慣了。那名婦人的年紀和媽媽不相上下，但福態很多，她穿著一件不成形狀的長裙和一件蓬鬆的 T 恤，一張臉漲得通紅。

假期中發生的倒霉事

- 你或你的家人曾經在假期中碰到過什麼麻煩事嗎？
- 想像如果你是傑可，你會怎麼做？

P.24

「我每年都會來希臘，我還第一次發生這種事，我一直覺得這裡很安全。」她說。

警察聳聳肩，說道：「這是個很安全的國家，不過現在這裡有很多外國人，如果去憲法廣場，一定要小心看好包包，不可以把包包放在椅背上。」

接下來，輪到了我。警察聽我投訴，不過顯然他認為我是在編故事。

「你爸爸不見了？」他問我。於是我做了番解釋。

「或許他只是忘了。」

我告訴他，爸爸是從克里特島來接我，而且他的衣服還在飯店裡。

「飯店的名稱叫什麼？」他問。

「依蕾皇宮飯店。」我回答。

這時警察露出有點驚訝的表情，顯然我的穿著看起來不夠拉風，不像是會住這種高級飯店的人。

他打了通電話給飯店，之後又去找了一位同事談。

「我們昨天已經打過電話給所有的醫院了，你父親並沒有進醫院，我不知道你還希望我們怎麼做？」他說。

其實我也不知道，當然，我希望他們可以找到爸爸，只是他們看起來不像那種會飆車辦案，就像電影裡頭聯邦調查局探員在尋找失蹤人物那樣。

P.26

我又開始說道：「是這樣的，我父親是考古學家亞歷克斯‧懷特，昨天下午，他離開飯店到機場接我，但現在卻不見了，你們應該可以處理一下吧？」

我很想再補充一句，我也是個走失的孩子，不知道該如何聯絡上媽媽，也不知道到底該怎麼辦才好，但我不想讓自己聽起來像個吃奶的小孩。不過，我好像說出了一個咒語。

「考古學家？」警察說道：「我知道了，你跟我來。」

我一頭霧水，警察也沒有加以說明，但至少他沒有打發我。他帶我到一個小房間裡，叫我坐下來，然後關上門離開。

這個房間裡的擺設很簡單，只有一張低矮的咖啡桌，上面放了一些咖啡杯，還有三張舊塑膠椅和兩個灰色的檔案櫃。我的假期一開始就這麼精彩，我心想。

「好了，傑可，凡事都要往正面想。」我告訴自己：「也許他在工作上出了什麼重大的事情，有重大的發現，爸爸一定要在現場。他正滿身泥土，準備進入現場，他一方面很過意不去，但另一方面也很興奮，因為可以帶我去看他發現的東西。」

又或者，他只是一時忘了，警方會在博物館裡一個積滿灰塵的房間裡找到他——但我停下這種的猜測，因為爸爸在電話或電子郵件上，看起來都不像是個會忘東忘西的人。

我就這樣一直打轉著，想不出什麼結果來。

VENUS FROM MILOS

P. 27

我又查看了一下手機，只收到了一則彼特傳的簡訊，他是我在學校裡的死黨。我開始回簡訊，但就在這個時候，

房間的門打開了，不過走進來的並不是爸爸，而是另一名警察。他說他叫尼寇斯·費洛什麼的，負責偵辦警局裡的考古案件。他比第一位警察來得年輕，看起來也一付更有效率的樣子，不過顯然他並不喜歡我，只是我看不出原因何在。

「你父親現在在進行什麼考古？」他問道。

我說我不知道，並解釋了一下。他看來有些驚訝，但什麼也沒說。

「你是負責偵辦考古案件的警察？」我問。

「我們希臘是人類文明的起源，有一些世界上最珍貴的寶物，有很多人想打它們主意，像是米洛的維納斯，或是被埃爾金伯爵帶到倫敦去的埃爾金大理石雕。」

P. 28

「你覺得我父親發現有人正在偷盜寶物？」

「這我不知道，但這個可能性永遠都存在，我當然會聯絡克里特島上的英國考古學院……」尼寇斯說。

「我想他在這裡也有辦公室。」我說。

「是在英國考古學院那裡，我認識他們。」他回答道：「你說他的行李還在飯店裡，你有徹底翻過他的東西嗎？有沒有文件或什麼東西的，可以看出來他曾去了哪裡？」

「沒有。」我說。

昨天我看了他的箱子一整晚，但要翻他的東西，讓我感覺像是在做壞事，畢竟我和他根本就不熟。不過今天早上，我實在厭煩透了，終於開了他的行李箱來看。裡頭沒有任何文件，事實上也沒有任何東西可以透露出父親的事。我不確定自己期待能找到什麼，一本日記？還是他的筆電？他有帶上筆電嗎？我不知道，箱子裡只有一般用品、一個清洗袋、一件汗衫，以及⋯⋯

攜帶的物品

- 你可以由一個人所攜帶的物品中看出這個人嗎？
- 你會把什麼東西放進自己的包包裡？

P.29

「事實上他的箱子裡有這個東西。」我跟尼寇斯說道。

我拿出一塊小石塊給他看，它的顏色看起來像黏土，上面有一些模糊的暗紅色斑點。

尼寇斯拿起石塊，在手上掂了掂重量。「這可能值錢，也可能不值錢。」他說：「我不像你父親那樣是位專家，不過我會把它送去實驗室，讓他們分析上面的塗料。這可能很古老，你父親也許有了什麼新的發現。」

他講話的樣子，好像這是很不可能發生的事情。

「你覺得有人想把它們從希臘偷渡出去？」

「什麼事情都是有可能的，但答案可能很簡單，我們等著瞧。」他笑笑地說

道，至少他的嘴巴是笑著的。

他的目光很冷峻，看起來很急躁、很不耐煩的樣子。

P.30

「在這期間，我想你應該回家，等我們找到他。」

於是我跟他說了媽媽的事。

尼寇斯說：「這的確是個棘手的問題，你得返回英國，我想我們要打個電話給你的大使館。」

他拿起話筒，和幾個人說過話。他說的話我完全聽不懂，只聽到他重複了幾遍的爸爸名字。接著，他站起身來，把話筒遞給我。

「這是你們的英國大使，亞歷克斯・懷特似乎和他很熟。」他說。

我心想，總算可以和一個認識爸爸的人講話了，我於是接過話筒。

「是傑可嗎？」一個慈祥而有教養的聲音說道：「我是約翰・帕森斯，你父親是我們全家人的老朋友，剛才費洛帕波斯督察已經告訴我是怎麼回了事，這一點也不像是亞歷克斯的作風。不過你不用擔心，我們一定會查個水落石出。你媽那邊我會打電話給她。」

我解釋無法聯絡上媽媽的箇中原委。

101

「好吧，」大使説：「那麼其他的家人呢？」他問道。

「我還有個阿姨在加拿大，」我説：「另外我爸爸有個弟弟，他在七歲那年就死於痲疹了。」

「那朋友呢？」大使問。

我想到了彼特，但又想起他和家人去了法國，我不知道他們現在到底在哪裡。

P.31

朋友和家人

• 如果你是傑可，你會聯絡誰？

「既然這樣，那你就來我這裡吧，我太太蘇西一定會很高興的，而且你也可以陪陪我女兒娜塔莉。你多大啦？十六歲嗎？」大使説。

「快了。」我説。

「那和小娜差不多大，她也才十八歲，有年紀相當的人作伴，她一定會喜歡的。」

要一個十八歲的女孩高高興興地去陪一個還未滿十六歲的毛頭小子，世界上有這種事嗎？在學校裡，要一個十二年級的女孩，樂於花時間去跟一個九年級、十年級的人在一起，簡直是不可能中的不可能。我猜想，娜塔莉一定是個聰明高傲的人，很快就會討厭我。

我向尼寇斯督察道別，我想他一定不會採取任何行動去尋找我爸爸。雖然他答應過，一旦有任何消息就會立刻通知我，而且還抄下了我的手機號碼，但我並不指望能夠再接獲他的消息。後來當我經過警察局的大辦公室時，我看到原先那位警員正在處理一位美國老先生的事情。

P.32

那位美國老先生説：「我只是出來散個步，我知道飯店附近有某種招牌，對面有一家咖啡廳。」

警員努力表現出一付很有耐心的樣子，在我們經過他的旁邊時，他向我揮了揮手，説道：「希望你可以找到你爸爸。」

另一名警員帶我回飯店。我收拾了自己的行李和爸爸的東西，然後去結帳。櫃枱人員向我表達了他的遺憾之情，好像他真的很難過一樣。

接著，我們驅車來到了英國大使館。那是一棟宏偉的建築，四周都是花園，外圍圍著圍牆。我心想不妙了，我只帶了幾件牛仔褲和 T 袖，我想待在這種房子裡面的人一定都是西裝筆挺的。

我心想，我這趟旅程徹頭徹尾是一場災難。然而，我才走向前面的階梯，就看到一位高高瘦瘦的婦女，她綁著馬尾，穿著一件髒牛仔褲和一件寬鬆的白色大襯衫，襯衫上還沾了紅色的泥巴。

「嗨，你一定是傑可了，」她説：「我叫蘇西，快進來吧！可憐的孩子，這真是一場惡夢。這太不像亞歷克斯的作風了，我還真想不透他到底發生了什麼事。我們一定要往好的方面想，大概只是工作的事讓他耽擱了。總之，歡迎你來到這裡，我們會把事情弄個水落石出的。」

她的人好親切，讓我感覺一見如故。

「幽靈和餓死鬼，娜塔莉戲稱其他國家的大使是餓死鬼。」

我跟著她走下一道長廊，心想她什麼時候會停止說話、喘口氣。

「你餓了嗎？」蘇西問我：「我們午餐比較晚吃，我習慣在上午把大部分的工作趕完，約翰有跟你說我是個陶藝家嗎？我下個月要舉辦一場展覽，因此得盡量多抽出些時間。我們到了……」她停止了說話，這時我們走進了一間英式農莊的廚房，裡面有一張很大的松木桌、幾張老舊的扶手椅子，椅子上有兩隻慵懶的肥貓。

P.35

「這裡就是我們生活的地方，如果由我來作主，我們每餐飯都會在這裡解決，不過因為我們代表國家，所以每個星期都要辦個幾次的正式餐會。不過你不必刻意裝扮、做社交，小娜就不肯這麼做。我也告訴她，她的作法沒錯，沒有人會管她是不是大使的女兒，所以啦，她都是在這裡用餐的——只要她進到這裡，就是要來找東西吃的。她晚上通常不在家，不是去夜店就是去咖啡廳。你知道她的生活就是那樣一回事。」

大使館和大使

・大使館是什麼？它為什麼很重要？
・大使又是什麼？
・想像如果是在大使館裡長大，那種生活會是什麼樣子的？會和你現在的生活有何不同？

P.34

「娜塔莉會帶你四處看看，她自己一個人剛從寄宿學校回來，要回來待幾個星期。小娜！」她回頭放聲喊道，「娜塔莉是我們的女兒，現在快進來吧，別站在那裡。」她繼續說道。

我們走進氣派的門廳裡，裡頭滿眼都是廊柱和大理石，好像皇宮一樣。石膏天花板裝飾得好像婚禮蛋糕，而且什麼聲音都會產生回音。

「在雅典這一帶地區，除了貝納基博物館，這裡大概是僅存的傳統式大建築物了，」蘇西邊走邊說道：「冬天時，暖氣的花費很高，不過還好夏天時很涼爽。邱吉爾在一九四四年時還來過這裡，他來確保希臘不會被蘇俄所接收。……小娜覺得這裡鬧鬼……你說呢，親愛的？」她一邊回頭，一邊說道，我想回答蘇西，我並不知道。在大使館裡長大、和其他嬌生慣養的大使小孩一起去上夜店，這種滋味我是一點也不懂的。我住在齊斯特菲，那裡並不是什麼夜店或咖啡廳之都，而且應該是遠在小娜的「社交雷達」之外，她連那個地方在哪裡都不會知道。我很清楚，我和娜塔莉一定是不對盤的。

P.37

就在這時，娜塔莉走了近來。你看過賽馬走進圍場的畫面嗎？馬看起來全身閃閃發亮，彷彿每個人都花了幾天的功夫來給牠擦亮似的，所以一副完美無瑕、閃閃動人、狀況絕佳的樣子，整個樣子就非常的對味。這就是娜塔莉的出場。她對我笑了笑，好像真的很高興見到我一樣。我感到，不管我的人生會如何變化，我都想把娜塔莉當成我的朋友。

「嗨，你就是傑可吧。我想我媽一開始就把所有的事情都跟你講了，但你應該什麼都不記得了吧。」她說。

我露齒笑了笑。我想我早就齜牙咧嘴地笑了吧，就像《愛麗絲夢遊仙境》裡的那隻柴郡貓一樣。我知道，自己看起來就像個白痴一樣。

「你和你爸爸長得很像。」娜塔莉說。

「是嗎？」我問。

「不過比較年輕啦……」娜塔莉笑道，「你要喝咖啡還是茶？我們得隨時備妥茶水，好招待那些登門拜訪、一臉煩躁的英國佬。我們會奉上一杯道地的英國茶，讓他們冷靜下來，這很管用。」

「我喝咖啡好了。」我說道。

娜塔莉於是開始把水倒進複雜的義式濃縮咖啡機裡，然後把咖啡機扣起來。我不住地想，她的動作是那麼地優雅。

「娜塔莉……這個……」我打開話匣子。

「叫我小娜就好了，只有陌生人才會叫我娜塔莉。」她說。

她沒有把我當成陌生人看待！

「你認識我爸爸亞歷克斯？」

P.38

「當然認識！我們在克里特島有一棟度假小屋，你爸爸常來我們那邊住。從我有記憶以來，我就認識你爸爸了。」小娜說。

既然這樣，他為什麼不帶媽媽和我去克里特島？就在我感到納悶之際，娜塔莉為我們各煮好了一杯咖啡。我們把貓從椅子上推開——大掃貓的興致——然後一屁股坐下來。

「那你現在打算怎麼辦？」小娜問我。

「你是指什麼？我能怎樣辦？」我說。

「你不去找你爸爸嗎？」她追問道。

「不，我怎麼找？只能交給警方了。」我說。

「你想警方真的會動員起來好好做調查嗎？」

我並不這樣認為，我感覺，警方把我打發走就好了，他們並不會採取任何行動。我自己的判斷是，他們認定了亞歷克斯·懷特不想和兒子過暑假，所以帶著女朋友躲去某個海島上逍遙了，那些警察搞不好現在正拿著這件事來當笑柄。但我沒有跟小娜透露這些想法，我對她的好感開始有一點點打折扣了。

「這個……」小娜一邊說，一邊彎起腰下那雙異常修長的腿，「是嗎？」

她或許是長得漂亮沒錯，但她已經惹惱我了。

「我不認為，當然不認為，我不覺得警方會採取任何行動。」我告訴她。

「所以呢？」

P.39

「所以怎樣？我又能怎樣？」我說。

「你可以自己去調查呀。」小娜說。

看來她不是太無聊，就是腦袋秀逗了。

「真是的。」我把聲音壓到最低，盡量不要尖叫出來，但不是很成功，「你建議我應該怎樣做？我來希臘還不到一天，不但一個希臘字都不會講，甚至連我爸長得什麼樣子都不清楚。」

「你不清楚……」

「對，我已經有五年沒見到他了，你滿意了嗎？」

令人吃驚的事

· 傑可的事情讓小娜很吃驚。你想傑可此時作何感受？而小娜又是什麼樣的感覺？

· 你說過或聽過什麼令人吃驚的事嗎？請描述當時的情況。

只見她立刻換了語氣。

「傑可，很抱歉，我不知道有這種狀況。只是因為我很喜歡亞歷克斯，而且這並不是他的作風。他人真的很好，而且很體貼別人。」

「那他為什麼沒有去接機？」我拉高了講話的聲調問道。

P.40

「這我也想不通，」她說：「所以我才想我們得採取行動。」她的口氣聽得出來她真的很擔心。

「我們？」

「如果你不會講希臘話，對雅典也不熟，那你就需要我了。還是說，你只要像個傻瓜呆呆坐在這裡喝咖啡就好了？」

「我當然不想這樣。」我回答，並且盡量表現出積極和聰明的樣子，但喝杯咖啡怎麼會像起傻瓜？不過，要怎樣做才能在喝咖啡時不至於像個布丁一樣？
「那我們要從哪裡開始？」我問。

　我很懷疑她會有想法，不過這樣起碼可以不讓她繼續指責我什麼事都不做。我來這裡才一會兒的時間，她卻講得好像我已經好幾天都拿不出辦法來。

　「亞歷克斯失聯前所做的最後一件事，是搭上計程車，所以我們可以從這裡著手。大部分的飯店都和同一家計程車行合作，對不對？」

　看來是我錯了，她是有想法的，而且分析正確。

　「當然，是飯店幫忙叫計程車的。」我說。

　「你有那家飯店的電話號碼嗎？」

　我從口袋裡掏出飯店開立的收據，然後交給她。

　「我用我的手機打，這裡的電話不知道有多少人會聽到。」她說。

　「你是說大使館的電話受到監聽？」我問她。

　「沒錯，這是他們一貫的伎倆。媽媽說，在以前，如果你想跟政府表達什麼，那你只要隨便打電話找個人講，你想講的話就可以直達憲法廣場。」她說。

P. 41

　我覺得自己來到了一個很不一樣的世界。小娜拿出一個很薄的粉紅色手機，撥了飯店的號碼，和電話那頭的人喋喋不休地談了起來，她的希臘話聽起來很溜。我的意思是，在她說希臘語時不會帶著英國腔。

　「你有筆嗎？」她問。

　於是我遞給她一支筆和一張小紙條，

她在上面抄下了一個電話號碼。

　「太好了。」說完她就撥了號碼。

　這次她和電話那頭的人爭執了一會兒。「他們不肯把我的電話轉給那位司機。」她邊說，邊用手遮住手機。

　「還是說，我們請那位司機載我們到什麼地方去，你看怎樣？」

　「當然可以。」她說完，便又繼續講手機。

　「太好了，」她說完後闔上手機，然後放到口袋裡，「司機午餐過後會過來，我們可以叫他載我們去亞歷克斯下車的地方。現在我先帶你去你的房間看一下。」她又補充道。

P. 42

　午餐真是讓我大開眼界，但我指的不是食物。食物當然是沒話講，有麵包、起司，還有蘇西只用五秒就搞定的一大盤希臘式沙拉，但我指的是這一家人的談話。

他們這一家人，每個人講起話來都滔滔不絕，然而他們卻又好像能同時聽到別人在講什麼，很有一個家的感覺。像我跟我媽，能夠聊上十句話就要偷笑了。當然，她生氣發飆的時候除外。

他們這一家人什麼都能聊，他們聊到蘇西要展覽的作品，小娜接著提到她在倫敦參觀過的阿茲提克陶器展，然後約翰又告訴我，我一定要去看國立博物館裡的黑陶作品，於是小娜又說她一定會帶我去參觀。後來，他們又聊到一些熟人，說著對方的近況。我靠著椅背坐挺，心裡想著，生活在這樣的家庭裡不知道是什麼樣的感覺。

P.43

「對了，傑可，你今天下午打算做什麼？」蘇西又把我帶回他們的談話中。

「你就讓他休息一下吧。」約翰說。

「我們可以打電話給瓦西利，看他可不可以幫我們開一下衛城的後門，這樣等觀光客都離開之後，傑可就可以去裡面參觀。到時候我們可以爬到利卡丘的山頂上，喝喝飲料，傑可也可以看看那邊的景色。」蘇西建議道。

「順便看看雅典的空氣污染有多嚴重、交通有多擁擠，」小娜對我笑了笑，說道：「他大概會比較想等亞歷克斯，和他一起去衛城。」她補充說道。

我很吃驚，她怎麼會知道我心裡正在想的事情。

P.44

了解

• 傑可覺得小娜很了解他心裡在想什麼。你覺得最了解你的人是誰？

• 你覺得你最了解的人又誰？

「這也是當然啦。既然這樣，要不要過幾條馬路，去國家藝廊或是拜占庭博物館逛逛？那只要幾分鐘就到了。」蘇西說。

「好主意，那裡有艾爾·葛雷柯的作品，你搞不好會喜歡。」約翰說。

我準備回答說我很喜歡艾爾·葛雷柯的作品。我媽媽是教藝術的，所以我有一點點接觸，不過我還來不及回答，蘇西就說她覺得那像是畫匠的作品，看起來很粗糙。

「我就喜歡那種味道，很有生命力，畫得很好，不像是畫匠畫的。不過，還是由傑可來決定吧。」約翰爭辯道。

他們跟我講話的樣子，好像我是他們的家裡的一份子一樣，讓我難以置信。對我來說，去看看展覽，然後喝點涼的，是很平常的事。

他們聊著天時，我不住地想著，如果我是和爸爸住的話，我的生活大概就會像現在這個樣子。不過接下來，我又對自己的這種想法啞然失笑起來。如果我是和爸爸住……他又不一定想跟我住，他連來機場接機都沒有！

P. 45

最後我們決定白天就偷個懶，晚上時再一起去喝個涼的。這樣也剛好能配合我和小娜的計畫，我們要先去查出爸爸下計程車的地方。

＊　＊　＊　＊　＊　＊

那個計程車司機叫做史匹洛，小娜才和他談了沒幾分鐘，他便對小娜一見如故，不但一直咧著嘴傻笑，而且還聊個不停。根據小娜的轉述，爸爸那天要去機場接我，但由於提早出門，所以就決定先去辦公室一下。

「他有沒有說為什麼？」我問。

小娜翻譯了我的問題。

「沒有說。」小娜轉述道。

然後史匹洛又開始說了些話，小娜一邊聽，一邊皺起了眉頭。

「史匹洛說，當他車子開到英國考古學院的外面時，他發現對面停了一輛黑色大轎車。在你爸爸下計程車時，黑色轎車裡有一個男人也跟著下車。你爸爸一看到那個人，就轉身拿了二十歐元給史匹洛，說他忘了些東西，等一下他會自己去伊凡站搭地鐵去機場。你爸爸說完，就跑進大樓裡了。」

P. 47

「那史匹洛就開車離開了嗎？」我問。

「對，你爸爸甚至還沒等史匹洛找零錢，就跑掉了。」小娜說。

「那麼看來我們得去英國考古學院一趟，看看他接下來可能去了哪裡。」我說。

「沒錯。我們走幾分鐘就到了。」小娜也表示贊成。

不過史匹洛好像很關心爸爸失蹤的事，堅持說要免費載我們去。

他的車子在一棟新古典風格的大樓前停了下來，然後跟我們指出那輛黑色轎車當時所停的地方。史匹洛在離開走前，塞了他的名片給我，要我找到爸爸之後，跟他說一聲。

我們走進大樓，接待室裡那位叫薇姬的漂亮小姐告訴我說，她有看到爸爸走進大樓。她想了片刻之後，又說她沒有看到他離開。

她打了幾通電話，但回報說沒有人有看到他。看來他不是回來找人，也沒有去圖書室。小娜問，如果他沒有從這裡走出大樓，那還有別的出口嗎？

「有，從花園那邊可以走出去，只不過為什麼要走那邊？」薇姬說。

小娜和我彼此對望了一眼，我們都在想：一定是因為黑色轎車裡的那個人。

「我們可以去走那條路看看嗎？我們走到大門那邊，就會回來了。」小娜問。

P.48

「當然可以，有任何需要幫忙的地方，請盡管開口。這件事很奇怪，

我會打電話去克里特，看看那裡有沒有人有他的消息。」薇姬說。

「那可不可以順便問問他們，他現在在進行什麼案子？」小娜問。

「沒問題。雖然我不知道這兩件事有什麼關係。」薇姬說。

「你知道我在想什麼嗎？」當我們走進花園，穿過一個網球場時，我說：「警察曾經問我，爸爸有沒有把什麼文件帶在身邊。我在飯店裡沒有找到什麼文件，他會不會是把文件帶在身上？」

「有可能，或是把文件放在他的筆電裡，你爸爸都會隨身帶筆電。」小娜回答。

「文件一定是放在什麼地方了。」我說。

我們開始在四處打量，四周是樹木和一些灌木叢，沒有可以藏東西的地方。我們走到大門邊，然後再循著原路折返。

「在走廊的那面牆上不是有些櫃子嗎？」我想起了那排木門，不由得問道。

於是我們靜悄悄地開始打開所有的櫃子。櫃子裡幾乎塞滿了檔案、箱子和書籍，其中一個櫃子裡放了一個瓶子，瓶子裡裝了幾小片的陶器碎片。

「是『碎陶片』，『碎陶片』是古物陶器碎片的正式名稱，」小娜解釋道：「亞歷克斯說，就算是他們也無法把這些碎陶片拼起來，但也不允許把碎陶片扔掉。」她笑道：「這也是當然的啦，這些碎陶片有可能是二千年前的古物了。」

我想拿一塊小小的碎陶片，塞進自己的口袋裡，但我又想到此行的目的，就放棄了這樣的想法。

P. 50

「這和爸爸隨身攜帶的那一塊碎片很不一樣。」我說。

「是什麼樣的碎片？」小娜問。

於是我跟她提了有紅漆的那一塊粗石，她聽完皺起了眉頭。

「這聽起來和我看過的陶片都不一樣，陶器通常是很光滑的。」她說。

後來我們又發現三個吱嘎作響的舊櫃子。爸爸的筆電放在裡頭的一個帆布袋子裡，小娜一眼就認出來。她遠比我還了解我爸爸。

我們向薇姬道謝後便告別。薇姬沒注意到小娜多提了一個包包離開，還說一有我爸爸的消息，就會打電話到大使館。

我們走回通往大使館的那條陡坡上，盡量裝出一付若無其事的樣子。我整個腦海裡想的都是那台筆電，我迫不及待想看裡頭有什麼東西，我想我們一定可以在裡面找到線索。

我開始覺得小娜說的沒錯，爸爸一定是發生了什麼事，而不是因為他不想看到我。但這也不是什麼開心的感覺，爸爸如果安然無恙，就應該會打電話給我，難道不會嗎？現在的情況很奇怪，黑色轎車裡的那個人是誰？爸爸為什麼一看到他就要跑掉？

蘇西和約翰都在忙著工作，所以家用廚房裡空無一人。這個家用廚房是蘇西設計的，布置得可以讓他們一家人覺得不是住在大使館裡頭。

P. 51

當然，爸爸的筆電要有密碼才能打開，我們猜不著密碼是什麼。我們先是試了克里特島上的幾個考古區，像是 Knossos、Phaistos、Gortys，小娜也在網路上搜尋了一番，找到了 Armeni 和 Phylaki，可是都失敗。

密碼

- 你猜得到傑可父親的電腦密碼嗎？
- 你有密碼嗎？你的密碼是怎麼來的？

「沒有用的，什麼字都可以當密碼。」我說。

就在我們打算再試其他的名字時，傳來了說話聲，接著電話鈴聲大作。之後約翰和蘇西走了進來，我們見狀立刻把電腦闔上，但他們太忙了，沒有注意到我和小娜在做什麼。

「傑可，小娜，感謝老天，你們兩個都在這裡，剛才出了一點事了。」蘇西叫道。

「出了什麼事了？是有人放了炸彈嗎？」小娜問。

「不是，不是，沒那麼嚴重，」小娜父親的話有安定人心的力量，「是一個愚蠢的英國足球員啦。」

「誰？」小娜問。

「菲爾·達森！」蘇西提到這個炙手可熱的英國足球隊長，這是一個每家小報每天大概都會出現的大名。

「他好像是放假時開遊艇去克斯島附近玩，然後上岸吃午餐，這個時候來了一大堆狗仔隊，讓他很火大。」

「我們長話短說，」蘇西打斷老公的話，說道：「達森拿了酒瓶砸向一個攝影師，結果不小心砸傷了當地的一名警察，被收押了。」

「新聞界一定會瘋狂報導的。」小娜說。

「正是如此，」約翰點點頭說：「所以我們要達森太太來大使館這裡避風頭，全希臘大概只有這個地方可以讓她躲開那些攝影師。」

蘇西接著說：「約翰和我一直在討論這件事，」她轉頭向我說：「我們想如果她來這裡，那你最好迴避一下，傑可。」

原來如此，我以為他們喜歡我待在這裡，我還想像爸爸和我待在這裡的樣子，真是很愚蠢。他們想趕快把我打發走，我不知道自己將何去何從。我有一個老師或許會收留我，直到他們聯絡上我媽媽。我覺得自己實在夠悲哀的，所以差一點漏聽了蘇西結尾的發言。

「所以呢，你、小娜和我，我們今天晚上會搭船去希拉克翁，在那裡待上一陣子，你應該會喜歡的，我們的房子離海邊只有幾步遠……」

我眨了眨眼。他們並沒有要攆我回家，而且我還要和他們一起去……去……什麼地方來著？

「去希拉克翁？」我問。

「對，那在克里特島上，我們的房子就位在帕諾茂，沿希拉克翁的海邊走二十分鐘就到了。英國的記者會守在我們的門口，這樣我沒辦法工作。」蘇西說。

小娜笑了笑，說：「媽媽在克里特島上有

個燒陶的窯，她總是會找各種理由離開雅典，這樣就可以去她那裡的工作室工作了。」她悄悄地告訴我。

P.54

克里特島，我想的就是這個地方，這是爸爸工作的小島。或許我們可以在那裡查出爸爸現在在忙的案子，搞不好他人已經回到克里特島了，我們也許會找到他。我很興奮能去克里特島，但我也很難過爸爸不在這裡。這種思念的感覺就像我回到十歲時，代表學校的足球隊出賽或參與話劇演出一樣。

我應該很高興能去克里特島了，但我並沒有，因為我太想念爸爸了。此時此刻，我已經十六歲了，快十六歲了，但那種感覺卻還是跟十歲時一樣，我覺得好愚蠢。

幾天的時間晃眼即逝，還是沒有爸爸的消息。我心裡認定，他一定是改變心意，不想見到我了。我想蘇西一定也有這種感覺，只有小娜認定爸爸一定是出事了。為了討好小娜，我繼續試各種密碼進入爸爸的電腦。希臘的所有地名我們大概都試過了，但都沒有成功。

這天上午，英國考古學院的薇姬突然打電話來，告訴我們爸爸是在馬他拉附近的一個地方工作。又因為他的一位同事不在，所以這個消息才拖這麼久才傳到我們耳裡。

小娜看了看地圖，告訴我說：「你一定會喜歡馬他拉的，媽媽在六〇年代時常往那個地方跑，那裡有很多奇異的洞穴，很多嬉痞都跑去那邊住。那裡是宣揚愛和和平之類的活動中心，瓊妮·米歇爾還為那個地方寫了一首歌。」

我笑了笑，有時候小娜說話的樣子跟她媽媽好像。

「她就是在那裡認識亞歷克斯的。」她繼續說道。

「誰？瓊妮·米歇爾？」我問。

P.55

「不是，是我媽，你不知道嗎？她和亞歷克斯有過一段情。」小娜說。

「和我爸爸？」

這個讓我吃驚的消息，說明了許多事情，像是我媽為什麼那麼痛恨希臘，又為什麼我從沒在克里特島見過約翰和蘇西。其實只要有誰比她早認識爸爸，她就一律對他們充滿敵意，好像爸爸的生命中只能有她一樣。

「是啊，這是好多年前的事了，她比你媽媽更早認識你爸爸，他們後來一直是好朋友。你媽媽把你爸爸趕出來之後，你爸就住在這裡。」

爸爸和蘇西！

「你想去馬他拉嗎？」我說。

「想啊，為什麼不去？我們可以在紅灘露營，媽媽不會反對的。我們或許可以在那裡找到線索。」

我打開爸爸的筆電，想再試最後一次，小娜在一旁看著我。

「用你的名字呢？」小娜建議道。

「用我的名字？」我說。

「試試看。」她說。

「我的名字太短了。」我跟她說。

「那就再加上你的生日。」她說。

我於是鍵入了「Jake1304」，那是我的生日，四月十三日。賓果！

個陌生人都想像成是國際珠寶大盜。那輛車子搞不好是某個大使的用車，那個男人只是前來拿一些資料。爸爸只是突然變卦，想去學校找女朋友罷了。我真是個白痴。我的心情又整個翻過來，好像有一隻黑狗趴在我的背上一樣。

我打開檔案，上面有一張小地圖，還有一些文字和數字。

「Melissa，」小娜看著地圖，說道：「那是一個地方的名字，在馬他拉附近。」

一個地方！那隻黑狗跳了下來跑走了。

p. 58

心情

- 什麼事情會讓你有好心情？什麼事情又會讓你心情不好？
- 傑可說他的心情很差，好像有一隻黑狗趴在背上一樣。回想一下你心情不好的時候，你會怎麼形容那樣的心情？
- 再想一下心情愉快的時候，你又會如何形容愉快的心情？

小娜研究著螢幕上的地圖，和她那張克里特島的地圖比對了一下，然後用手指指著島嶼南端突出來的一個陸岬。

「這裡是最南端了，再過去就沒有了，可以直達非洲。」她說。

「這些文字和數字是什麼？」她問。

「我猜是羅盤上的數據。」我說。

「當然，爸爸出海航行時都會用到。那你怎麼會知道？」她說。

P. 57

我驚訝地瞪著螢幕，看著電腦圖示彈出來。沒有陪伴在我身邊的這麼長的日子裡，爸爸還是使用我的名字和生日，這對他來說看似很重要。我不想讓小娜看出我的感受。

「我們打開 Word 檔，看會跳出哪些檔案。」小娜說。

我按下 Word 檔的圖示，歷史檔案中只有一個文件，檔名是 Melissa。小娜把身體靠向我，她的頭髮碰到了我的臉，我聞到了蘋果的香味。

「Melissa？那是女生的名字，對吧？」小娜說。

Melissa！我最初的直覺沒有錯，爸爸交了新的女朋友，女朋友要比未成年的兒子有趣。我和小娜發現的什麼黑色轎車的事，都只是我們想像出來的。我們不過像是讀了偵探小說的小孩，把每

113

「我常去健行和爬山，我們家就住在山谷區旁。」我告訴她說。

「真的？」她問。

「真的。」我說道。我知道她對我住的地方一無所知。我看著地圖補充道：「那裡看起來像是在很高的斷崖邊。」

p. 59

「沒錯，所以才有很多洞穴啊，笨蛋。」小娜說。

「妳才是笨蛋！是誰連羅盤的數據都看不出來的？」我反駁道。

小娜用拳頭在我的肩頭上捶了一下，活像個姊姊似的。我心想，我沒有姊妹，但是我幻想能有個姊妹。而小娜，她應該是最好的那種姊姊了。

他們在帕諾茂的那間房子，是那種讓人想住下去的房子。每個房間裡都可以找到上次度假時所留下的有趣玩意兒。其中有一堆堆褪色的海浴巾，還有大概是掉進海裡、被水泡皺的的書。

p. 60

我在一個角落裡看到了一些登山的設備，有人用過後就把它扔在那裡。小娜沒有爬過山，所以我們也不能用它來做什麼，不過我習慣把東西準備好，於是就撿起一些繩子、一個羅盤，並且備妥了一些火把和備用電池。

小娜笑了起來，直叫我童子軍。我是在我家附近的山谷區救過一些人沒錯，那些人什麼該帶的設備都沒帶。

第二天一大早，我們出發前往 Melissa。克里特島和我想像中的不一樣，也不像其他的島嶼那樣。克里特島比較大，而且沿途的景色一直在變化。他們在帕諾茂的房子位在斷崖上，臨著小海灣，海水是深綠色的，不過在其他地方的海灘都很長，海水非常的湛藍。

我們開著車子一路往南駛去時，沿途的景色不停地變化著，有小村莊，有溪水奔流的深谷，讓我不禁想起了自己的家鄉，接著是綿延數英哩的山岩，看起來有點像月球表面。

p. 61

我們開著車經過一個種滿葡萄樹和橄欖樹的谷地，那裡四處點綴著年久失修

的舊房子。這時，我看到了一張熟悉的面孔。那個人正坐在一家咖啡廳外面，在和兩個男人談著話。我連忙別過頭去，不過我想是來不及躲開了，他一定看到了我。

「怎麼了？」小娜問。

「是尼寇斯，他是我在雅典遇到的那位警察局督察。」我說。

「他來這裡做什麼？」她問。

「我也不知道，你想他會知道我爸爸在哪裡嗎？」

「我不知道，不過這可以證明我說得沒錯，一定是發生了什麼事情。」她說。

我們決定按照爸爸的羅盤數據來追蹤，靠著約翰的一張航海圖，我們覺得那些數據顯示出是位在 Melissa 的東邊，位在馬他拉和一個叫做卡利的小地方之間。但問題來了，那裡沒有路可以到，而且我們也沒有船。

p. 62

「我們可以把車停在卡利，然後就用走的過去。」小娜說。

「這裡好像有一條小路，」我指著地圖說：「從這裡可以往上走到一間修道院，到了那裡有另外一條小路可以朝著 Melissa 走到海邊。」

事實上我們找到了一條新闢的小道，走上一小段，然後轉進小路。這裡的路不好走，有很多小石子和長刺的草叢。我們踏上一條大概是羊群走的通道，沿著山脊前進，最後來到了一處空地上。前面沒有路了，腳下就是大海。

「有人來過這裡。」小娜說。

「他來這裡做什麼，這裡什麼都沒有。」我問。

我們解下背包喝點水，我的水壺這時朝一大片長刺的草叢滾下去，我追過去，水壺停在草叢後面，那裡有一個洞穴入口。

「這就是他來這裡的原因。」小娜說。

「你是說我爸爸？你覺得他在這裡？」我問。

「當然，他在勘察這些洞穴。」她說。

我們走回放背包的地方，拿出火把，走進洞穴開始探查起來。洞穴的入口看起來好像才剛被挖大過，但洞穴其實很小，裡頭的通道很窄，還架著一些岩架。

115

p. 64

「裡頭的洞穴不只一個。」小娜說。

「沒錯,」我同意道:「這裡有很多洞穴,有通道相通,我們要在牆上做記號,這樣才能認出回頭的路。」

「我不喜歡這裡,好冷。」小娜說。

洞穴

• 你進過洞穴裡嗎?你為什麼會進去(或是沒進去)?

• 傑可和小娜決定進入洞穴一探究竟,你覺得用下列哪些形容詞來形容他們是最貼切的?

☐ 勇敢　☐ 愚蠢　☐ 魯莽　☐ 聰明

「你看,有亮光了,我們找到另一個出口了。」我說。

「真是謝天謝地。」當我們腳步蹣跚地穿過通道,步出洞穴、重見光明後,小娜說道。

我們穿過了一座山,來到了另一頭。我們現在置身在山谷的後方,闖進了一塊農地的中間。這裡看起來很荒涼,只有幾間看起來還滿新的鐵皮屋,上面鎖著的大掛鎖看起來也很新,超新的。

p. 65

緊接下來,發生一連串的事情。

小娜大叫一聲:「傑可!」不過我沒聽她在說什麼。

就在那一瞬間,我確定我看了爸爸。我拔腿就跑,大聲叫喊著,跑到一間鐵皮屋前,然後往牆上猛敲,大叫著:「爸!爸!是我!我是傑可!」

這大概是我這輩子做過最蠢的事了。我是說,你要如何讓綁匪知道你已經發現他們了?答案就是大喊大叫,製造噪音。

那些人一下子就從鐵皮屋裡跑出來,沒兩三下就抓住我和小娜。他們持著槍,把我們推進鐵皮屋裡。他們看到我們,心裡很不悅。

他們惡狠狠地朝我的臉揍了一拳,我一個踉蹌跌倒在地,接著他們又用槍抵住小娜的腦門。他們要我説清楚來歷，不然小娜就沒命。我據實以告，但並沒有説小娜是英國大使的女兒。不知怎麼地，我騙他們説，小娜是我的姊姊，我們雖然驚魂未定，但我看到小娜微微笑了一下。

p. 66

那些人看來是相信了我的話，他們走到一旁竊竊私語。他們一共有五個人，其中有兩個像是老大，講著我聽不懂的語言。另外三個人我猜是北非人。看來他們唯一的共通語言是英語，不過我不是很聽得懂他們在講什麼。我只聽到一些像是「等等看」和「已經晚了」的字眼，還聽到了「巴米爾」這個名字。此外，我還聽出了「考古學家」這個字，我想他們一定是在談爸爸的事。我開始在想他們可能已經把他殺了，我頓時感到一陣嘔心。

小娜走過地板朝我靠過來，然後緊緊握住我的手。我很想擠出一絲笑容，但我的下巴很痛。我在想能不能拿到我的手機，不過其中有一個傢伙也想到了這一點，於是奪走了我們的背包和手機。

p. 67

不過他們現在好像沒有多餘的時間來處置我們。他們把我們的手腳反綁，然後把我們推進後面的一個房間裡。看來是有什麼可怕的事情在上演，我很害怕，幾乎無法思考。還好的是，小娜還能思考。

「我們得想辦法離開這裡，這裡太危險了。你有辦法移動嗎？」小娜小聲説。

危險

- 如果是你置身在這樣的處境中，你會如何處理？
- 你曾經遇過什麼危險的情況嗎？那是怎麼一回事？你當時是怎麼處理的？

我側著身子慢慢朝著小娜挪過去，嘗試用牙齒想咬斷綁在她手腕上的繩子。在電影裡，這種事看起來很簡單，實際上是很困難。我慢慢地努力咬鬆第一個結，然後把結打開。第二個結咬起來輕鬆些，在一陣努力之後，我終於鬆綁了小娜手上的繩子。

小娜很快解開她腳踝上的繩子，然後鬆開我身上的繩子。這個房間裡有一扇小窗戶，窗戶面對著田地旁的山腰。在我們準備打開窗戶時，發現窗戶吱嘎作響，我們於是趕緊住手，心想會有人衝進來。

p. 68

不過當我們打開窗戶時，卻聽到了一陣可怕的嘈雜聲，那是一個女人的尖叫聲，從鐵皮屋裡頭傳出來。

「我們究竟闖進了什麼鬼地方啊？」小娜悄聲問道。小娜說出了我心裡的話，尖聲的女人是誰？還有，爸爸到底在哪裡？

我們知道我們不能回鐵皮屋，也不能走到田地的前面，所以我們只能往山上走。我們慢慢爬出窗戶，由我先往下跳，小娜緊跟在後。不過小娜在跳下來的時候扭到了腳踝，摔了一下。

我連忙幫她扶起，她的臉色變得很蒼白。我很擔心，怕她會摔斷了腿。

「你的腳還可以移動嗎？」我問道。

她點點頭，「我想只是扭到筋，腳踝的筋。」

鐵皮屋裡的那些人正忙著，沒有看到我們正在山坡上的刺叢間攀爬。等我們爬到快到山頂時，才發現他們為什麼不需要在山上設農場的柵欄了，因為山頂上的另一側是斷崖，高度約有三十公尺高，下面是扁平的岩石，再過去的斷崖下方就是大海了，而我們的繩子被那些人拿走了。

「我們得從另外一邊走回去。」小娜說。

我開始仔細端詳那邊的斷崖，它並沒有想像中的陡峭，可以攀爬下去。

「我們不能回去，他們會殺了我們的，我們一定要爬下去。」我說。

「可是我想我連站都站不起來。」小娜說。

「我可以揹你下去。別擔心，要爬下去不是太難，我可以的。」我說。

p. 69

我說這話時覺得非常難受。我還沒自己一個人在沒有繩子的情況下爬下過這種陡坡。不過，我們沒有別的選擇。我坐下來，讓小娜爬到我背上。

「我揹得比你重的行李，」我邊站起來，邊說道：「我需要你盡量趴平在我背上。」

「好。」她在我的頸子邊悄聲說道。

「千萬不要往下看喲。」我又補充道。

「我沒辦法往下看的。」她說道。

就這樣我開始慢慢往下爬，一次只移動一隻腳或一隻手。我第一次不帶設備爬這種岩壁，不過這也不是不可能的事，只要知道怎樣緊握住每個支撐點就可以。不過只要一個失手或失足，就會摔落下去。

「別想東想西的，」我對自己說道：「只要集中精神在支撐點上就好了，一個一個來。」

岩石又乾又硬，不會碎裂，也不會很滑。「只要做下去就對了，」我對自己說：「一定可以的。」

就這樣我一步一步地往下爬，每抓住一個支撐點，整隻手臂就一陣疼痛。我爬下斷崖，感覺好像爬了好幾個鐘頭之久。但最後，我終於感到我的腳踩在扁平的岩石上了。我又可以喘氣了，我完成了。

「我們安全了。」我說。

小娜哭了起來，我抱住她，這樣她才不會發現我也哭了。

過了一會兒，我們開始思考下一步該怎麼辦才好。在我們下方的岩石更陡峭，掉下去就會直接落海。這次沒有繩子我是下不去的，何況還要背著小娜。

p.70

「如果有船經過，也許會看到我們。我如果沒打電話給媽媽，媽媽就會開始找我們，他們會派出直升機來找我們。」她說。

這時，我們聽到了聲響，是從山的另一頭傳來的，聲音有點微弱，不過我們聽得出來那是什麼聲音。

「是槍聲嗎？」我問。

我想到那個尖叫的女人和爸爸，不禁渾身打冷顫。一會兒後，槍聲停止了，只聽得到海濤聲和風聲。

「這裡好像還有一些洞穴，我進去看一下，如果我們晚上要在這裡過夜，可以有地方待。」我說。

這裡的洞穴入口看起來好像也是才剛被開鑿過。我一進入洞內，很驚訝地看到裡頭放了很多的備用物品，有好幾瓶水、一個火把、紙張和一些火柴。

我帶著水，幾乎用跑地回小娜那裡。小娜堅持要和我一起去洞穴裡頭看看，於是我扶住她，她一拐一拐地走著。

「看來有人在這裡工作。」她說。

「你想是那些人嗎？」我問。

她搖搖頭，「那些人看起來不像是會爬山的人，我想，是亞歷克斯。」

我舉起火把，一起往洞穴裡走進去。接著，我們看到了它們，它們布滿了牆面，那是動物和人類的畫像。那些人類手持長矛，拿著像是石器的東西，就像

拉斯科洞穴裡的壁畫一樣。真是令人難以置信，那些繪畫燦爛奪目，看起來就像紅色的火焰一般。

p.72

「這就是爸爸發現的東西。」我說道。

「這表示，他也發現了那個農場，也就是說……」小娜說。

小娜並沒有把話說完。我們想到了剛才的那陣槍響，於是忍住不要哭出來。

這時，我又聽到了一聲音傳來。

「有人來了。」我說。

我們環顧四周，四周就這樣了，沒有地方可以躲，也不能往上走或是往下走。

小娜抓住我的手，說道：「傑可，我只是想說……」

119

最後的話

· 你覺得小娜想對傑可說什麼？
  寫下來和夥伴分享。

不過我還是不知道她想對我說什麼，因為這時我聽到有人在呼喊她的名字，還有我的名字。

「是亞歷克斯嗎？」小娜小聲地問。

「是爸爸嗎？」我也小聲問道。

接著我們放聲大喊了起來：「亞歷克斯！爸爸！我們在這裡！」

這麼多年來我一直渴望見到的人，此刻就在我的眼前，他緊緊地抱住我們，哭了起來。我們也哭了，緊緊地抱住他的背。

p. 74

他把小娜抱到洞穴外面，這樣我們就可以坐下來說話。

「我們要再等一下，等警察來清理現場，然後我們再走洞穴回去。」他說道。

「這個洞穴也通到農場嗎？」我問。

爸爸點點頭，「我在幾個星期前發現了這個洞穴。我在這裡工作了幾個月了，但一直到幾個星期前才發現這個洞穴。實在令人難以置相，歷史要改寫了，我們還不知道這裡在這麼早以前就有人類居住了。」

「那麼那座農場……？」小娜問。

「那是什麼農場？」我問。

「那是用來走私人口的地方，他們用船把非法移民載過來，然後走這些洞穴進到農場裡。除了這裡之外，他們還會利用海平面上的另一處洞穴。」爸爸說。

「警方為什麼不逮捕他們？」小娜問。

「警方已經來抓人了，你們沒聽到槍聲嗎？」爸爸說。

「那是警方開的火？」我問。

「對，警方一直在等頭頭出現，他們想揪出後面的藏鏡人。」爸爸轉向我說：「傑可，很抱歉，事情變得一團亂，我以為我做的事情是對的，但我現在知道自己通通錯了。」

「那你為什麼不先跟我說？」我問。

「警方要我先離開洞穴，我以為那些人口販子沒有注意到我，可是在我要去機場的路上時，我才發現他們在跟蹤我。」

p. 75

「就是黑色轎車裡的那個人。」小娜說。

爸爸說：「我當時很驚慌，我不想讓他們知道有你這個人，他們很殘暴的。」他補充說道：「我那時希望你趕快返回英國。」

「但是尼寇斯督察沒告訴你，我暫時回不去嗎？」我問。

「沒有，他沒說，」爸爸嚴肅地說道：「他一直到今天才說，他看到你們開著車經過龐比亞，猜想你們會來這裡，才打電話給我，然後我就直接趕過來了，幸虧及時……」

＊　＊　＊　＊　＊　＊

不久後，爸爸的手機響了，他在電話中表示一切都安全了。

他抱起小娜，穿過洞穴，走回到停滿了警車的農場。

小娜接著被送往醫院去，幸虧她只是扭到筋。亞歷克斯回家後，把整件事情的經過一遍又一遍地告訴蘇西和約翰。他們聽得很吃驚，並且直呼我很勇敢，還表示他們不會生氣。

p. 76

現在我們就坐在帕諾茂的露臺上啜飲著咖啡，聊著接下來的假期安排。突然，我意會到，他們把我當成一份子算進去了。他們要我和爸爸陪他們再去克里特島玩。

就在大家說說笑笑之際，傳來了一個聲響。是尼寇斯督察，他出現在我們眼前。

「很抱歉，昨天有一個歹徒逃跑了，他正在跟蹤你們。」他說。

「那現在抓到他了嗎？」蘇西臉色蒼白地問。

「抓到了，現在你們安全了，他是最後要抓的歹徒，你們真的可以好好享受你們的假期了。」尼寇斯說。

我們確實是好好享受了我們的假期。爸爸帶我們回洞穴，我們要趁那些壁畫被攝影封存，然後用玻璃跟民眾隔離起來之前，好好再看最後一眼。爸爸給了我一小片一萬七千年前的紅土畫作，可是我並不需要，因為我已經有爸爸了。

ANSWER KEY

Before Reading

Page 6

1
1. b   2. b   3. c   4. a
5. a   6. c   7. b

Page 8

3
a) 7   b) 8   c) 5   d) 2
e) 6   f) 1   g) 3   h) 4

Page 9

4
1. islands   2. cliff   3. bay
4. ravines   5. streams   6. vines
7. olive   8. rundown

7
a) thriller
b) smuggling, a disappearance

Page 11

10
a) 7   b) 8   c) 5   d) 2
e) 6   f) 1   g) 3   h) 4

11
a) pottery   b) cave   c) compass
d) rope   e) padlocks   f) tabloids
g) earth paintings   h) cliffs

Page 12

13
a) In the middle of the Acropolis.
b) Greece.
c) Alexander Wyatt.
d) 5 years ago.
e) At Athens airport.
f) The traffic.
g) Syntagma Square.
h) The Acropolis.

Page 35

• An embassy is the house of the official government representative of a country in a foreign country. It is important because it represents the country abroad. The laws of the country of the embassy are valid inside the embassy.
• An ambassador is the official government minister who represents one country in another country.

After Reading

6

a) 15.
b) His mother.
c) She is at a yoga place in Scotland.
d) Walking and climbing.
e) Jake really wants to see his father. He is confused and hurt when his father is not there to meet him.
f) Jake enjoys being with Nat's family.

7

a) Inspector Nikos
b) John Parsons
c) Susie Parsons
d) Nat
e) His father
f) His mother

8 (Possible answers)

talkative, kind, creative, resourceful, friendly, thoughtful

9

a) He thought she was going to be smart and snobby.
b) He thought this because he imagined that children growing up in an embassy were like this.
c) He changed his mind because she immediately treated him as a friend.

10

a) F   b) T   c) T   d) F   e) T
f) F   g) T   h) F   i) F

11

a) 4   b) 2   c) 5   d) 6
e) 1   f) 3   g) 7

14

a) They had a row because Jake found out that his mother was hiding his father's letters from him.
b) Jake found his father's luggage in the hotel room.
c) Inspector Nikos wanted Jake to go home until they found his father.
d) They found his laptop in a canvas bag in a cupboard at the British School.
e) He had to go to Crete because there were lots of journalists and paparazzi at the embassy.
f) Melissa is a place on Crete.
g) They are compass readings.
h) The cave led to a farm.
i) Jake started shouting.
j) They tied their hands and feet and locked them into a room.

k) She couldn't climb down the cliff because she had hurt her ankle.

Page 84

15

a) 5   b) 8   c) 1   d) 4
e) 3   f) 2   g) 7   h) 6

Page 85

17

a) 4   b) 6   c) 5   d) 3   e) 2   f) 1

Page 86

18

a) had to
b) didn't have to
c) didn't have to
d) had to
e) had to
f) didn't have to

19

a) wanted Jake to spend the summer holidays with him.
b) didn't want Jake to see his father.
c) wanted Jake to go back home.
d) wanted Jake to look for his father.

Page 87

20

a) were sent back
b) were taken
c) is sorted out
d) is haunted
e) were tied up

Test

Page 88

1

a) F   b) T   c) T   d) F   e) F   f) T
g) T   h) T   i) F   j) T   k) T   l) F
m) T   n) T   o) T

Page 89

2

a) Jake has never visited the Parthenon.
d) Jake's aunt lives in Canada.
e) Nat's mother is a potter.
i) Jake thinks that Melissa is the name of his dad's girlfriend but it is the name of a place.
l) Jake drops his bottle of water and they find the entrance to the cave.

Page90

4

a) F   b) T   c) F   d) T
e) F   f) T   g) T   h) F

Project Work

Page 92

1

a) 150
b) 11,000
c) 4,000

國家圖書館出版品預行編目資料

憂鬱少年的藍色希臘(寂天雲隨身聽APP版) /
Antoinette Moses 著；李璞良 譯. —初版. —[臺北
市] : 寂天文化, 2021.08印刷
　面；公分.
　中英對照
　ISBN 978-626-300-058-2 (25K平裝)
　1.英語 2.讀本

805.18　　　　　　　　　　　110013549

作者 _ Antoinette Moses
譯者 _ 李璞良
校對 _ 陳慧莉
封面設計 _ 蔡怡柔
主編 _ 黃鈺云
製程管理 _ 洪巧玲
出版者 _ 寂天文化事業股份有限公司
電話 _ +886-2-2365-9739
傳真 _ +886-2-2365-9835
網址 _ www.icosmos.com.tw
讀者服務 _ onlineservice@icosmos.com.tw
出版日期 _ 2021年8月 初版二刷
郵撥帳號 _ 1998620-0 寂天文化事業股份有限公司
訂購金額600 （含）元以上郵資免費
訂購金額600元以下者，請外加郵資65元
若有破損，請寄回更換

〔限台灣銷售〕